SEA TREK

SEA
TREK

Martha Holmes

BCA

LONDON · NEW YORK · SYDNEY · TORONTO

PICTURE CREDITS

This edition published 1991 by BCA
by arrangement with BBC Books,
a division of BBC Enterprises Limited,
Woodlands, 80 Wood Lane, London W12 0TT
First published 1991
© Martha Holmes 1991
CN 4458
Designed by Grahame Dudley Associates
Maps by Eugene Fleury
Cover Photographs by Georgette Douwma
Set in 11/15pt Sabon by Butler & Tanner Ltd, Frome, Somerset
Printed and bound in Great Britain by Butler & Tanner Ltd, Frome, Somerset
Colour separations by Tecknik Ltd, Berkhamsted
Jacket printed by Belmont Press Ltd., Northampton

'... Ocean, who is the creator of them all.'

Homer

ACKNOWLEDGEMENTS

The making of *Sea Trek* involved the help and advice of many people. Both the television series and the book have relied on information gathered by scientists and amateur naturalists over many decades. I am grateful to them all. In particular I would like to thank those scientists who have been directly involved in *Sea Trek* and who contributed a great deal: Denise Herzing, Russ Babcock, Johnston Davidson, Mary Stafford Smith, and Debbie and Mark Ferrari.

I am honoured to have been a part of the *Sea Trek* team. Mike deGruy, my co-presenter, was a marvllous companion, both above and below the water. His unrivalled ability to talk and amuse kept us smiling, sometimes under difficult situations. He too, shares a fascination for the animals that live in the sea, and his infectious enthusiasm was always refreshing. To Mike I am particularly grateful. Peter Scoones, Georgette Douwma, Denis Lomax, Andrew McClenaghan, Rob Brownhill, Andrew Penniket, Peter Thompson and Mike May all contributed to the excellence of the images. Mike Burgess ensured that Mike deGruy and I did not drown in the bubble helmets and patiently monitored our underwater conversations. Robin Hellier and Sara Ford directed us and guided us wisely. At each location we enlisted a boat crew, support divers and local expertise, all of whose generous assistance made the trips feasible, productive and enjoyable.

I would like to thank Kate Hubert for researching this book, and I am very grateful to Judy Maxwell and Peter Holmes for editorial assistance. Rupert Ormond kindly checked extracts for factual errors.

There are two others to whom I am especially indebted. Liz Appleby, although unable to come on location with us, provided constant encouragement throughout the project. William O'Kelly gave invaluable editorial advice and generous support during the writing of this book.

M H

CONTENTS

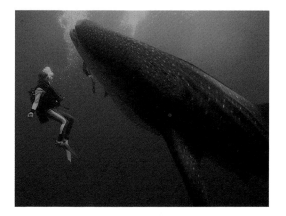

INTRODUCTION

As a child, my first swimming expeditions out of my depth took place on shores of the Middle East and were fraught with a fear of stingrays. Years later, secure in the knowledge that they eat small animals from the sandy ocean floor, I was happy to swim with them. In the Cayman Islands, stingrays gathered in their dozens around me and, for the first time, I felt their skin, rough on top but silky smooth underneath and I ran my hand over their poisonous spines. As with so many phobias, knowledge had overcome fear.

Man's quest for knowledge about what goes on under the surface of the sea is not new. There are tales of sea monsters, of great fish and also of man's excursions into this underwater world. Since Alexander the Great's fabled descent into the ocean in an unlikely sounding 'glass barrel' in 332 BC there has been a slow evolution of practical methods to enable us to explore the deep, one of the least accessible parts of the planet.

The development of scuba has allowed some people to experience the fascinating variety of life contained in the oceans. But to many, they remain vast watery wastelands, their gloomy depths still populated by a host of bizarre and monstrous creatures. Shallower seas present a friendlier face and, when bordered by sandy beaches and drooping palm trees, are nearer the popular conception of paradise. Even so, go beyond the turquoise shallows to the darker blue, and once again a dread of what is lurking below will stir many hearts. In the television series *Sea Trek*, and in this book which accompanies it, I have tried to reveal a little more of what really does happen under the seas and to convey some of the delight of this relatively unknown world. To achieve this my co-presenter Mike deGruy and the television production team visited what we felt to be some of the richest and most varied marine environments in the world. Our aim was to encounter the creatures that occupy these habitats and, in the event, we were able to spend time with all manner of invertebrates, fish, reptiles and mammals. We encountered humpback whales and swam with dolphins, sharks and sea otters. We could not, of course, match the power and agility of these animals, but a great deal of patience, combined with their curiosity, usually allowed us to get very close to them. We were extremely fortunate in being able to convey the immediacy of the encounters to our audience by using bubble helmets. These are heavy, uncomfortable and extremely hard work to dive in but, for all that, a great deal of fun, if only for the unrivalled opportunity they give for talking underwater.

The first diving location for both the programme and this book was the Galápagos archipelago off the coast of Ecuador. These isolated islands are home to many unique animals including the marine iguana; the only true marine lizard in the world. Although the islands lie in tropical water, a cold upwelling allows penguins and fur seals to thrive. From the Galápagos, we travelled to the Californian coast where kelp beds rival the state's giant redwoods in size and beauty. Instead of peering upwards, as in a land forest, we could explore all the kelp forest's life from the luxuriant canopy down to the seabed. Among the many animals we encountered there were enchanting sea otters, which wrap themselves in blankets of kelp at night, and dramatic-looking bat rays gliding gracefully through the maze of kelp. We also ventured out to the open ocean to swim with elegant and efficient hunters; the blue sharks.

Corals reefs are the richest ocean habitat, their complex framework offering living space to a host of creatures. This was amply demonstrated by the vast array of animals we found in the Great Barrier Reef, the largest structure built by any of Earth's creatures, including humans. We were particularly fascinated by the diverse techniques animals use to ensure successful reproduction. We observed the mass spawning of corals, fish that can change colour and sex, and turtles which swim thousands of miles to lay their eggs on a particular beach. We then went to the Caribbean on the other side of the world. Here we descended to the unlighted depths of a deep trench, passing on the way some of the brilliantly coloured sponges for which the area is famous. On shallower water we found stingrays and groupers, and spent many happy hours swimming with spotted dolphins.

Our final location was the most remote island group in the world, the Hawaiian chain. Despite having risen above the sea relatively recently and being so isolated, the islands have been colonised by a wide variety of marine and land animals, including humans. Over the past few decades, tourists have flocked to Hawaii and now the noise of pleasure boats mingles with the many sounds used by marine creatures to communicate, including the chirps, grunts and drumming noises of fish and the haunting song of the humpback whale.

The oceans of the world may seem too large and all encompassing to understand fully. However, in this book I will introduce you to some of the many creatures I encountered so that you too can delight in and enjoy a little of their wonder.

M H

THE GALÁPAGOS ISLANDS

Take five-and-twenty heaps of cinders dumped here and there in an outside city lot; imagine some of them magnified into mountains, and the vacant lot the sea; and you will have a fit idea of the general aspect of the Encantadas, or Enchanted Isles.

Herman Melville, writing in 1854 of his visit to the Galápagos Islands.

I, too, was struck by the desolation of the place: the barren landscapes, broken lava flows, the unforgiving stony ground. The harshness of this basalt wilderness was in stark contrast to the cornucopia of plants and animals I had expected. For the wildlife of the Galápagos Islands has been of enormous interest to zoologists since it was made famous by Charles Darwin, who used some of the islands' creatures as evidence for his theory of evolution.

Set in the Pacific Ocean, some 960 kilometres (600 miles) west of Ecuador to which they belong, the Galápagos Islands are very remote. It was not until 1535, when the Bishop of Panama unwittingly found himself drifting into the archipelago, that they were officially 'discovered'. Since then the islands have endured many a pirate and buccaneer, and more recently whalers and a smattering of hardy settlers. Today nature-loving tourists descend in their hordes.

An unexpected patch of green adorns the volcanic debris of the Galápagos Islands.

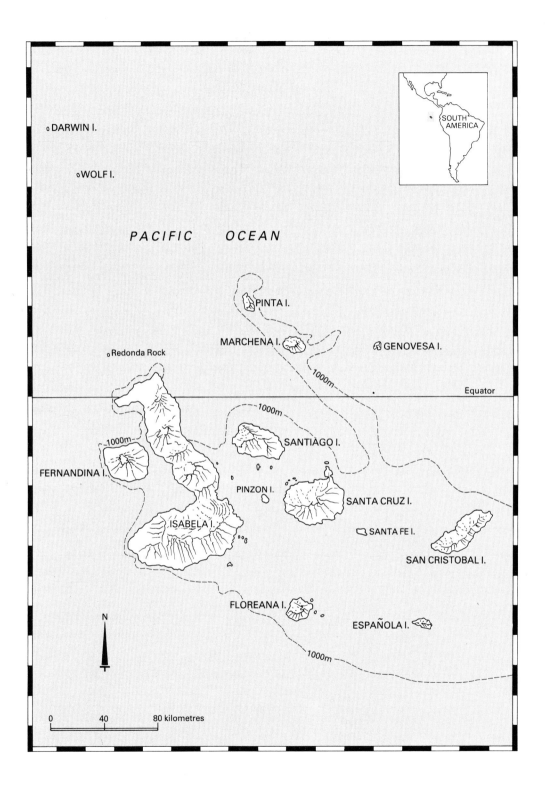

It is an impressive collection of volcanic islands, stretching 430 kilometres (270 miles) from Darwin Island in the extreme north-west to Española in the south-east. There are 13 main islands and over 65 small islets and rocks, many without names. Isabela, by far the largest, dominates the Galápagos skyline. It is made up of five volcanoes that were once separate islands and the remains of a sixth, all united by extensive lava flows to form a chain of craters. It boasts the highest peak in the archipelago at 1700 metres (5600 feet), though this, and indeed all the peaks, look more like rounded hilltops.

Harsh conditions prevail in the Galápagos. The bleakness of the landscape is partly due to the continuing volcanic activity, which makes the ground an uncertain place for plants and animals alike to colonise. Also, despite straddling the equator, the islands do not generally have the hot, humid climate typically encountered in the tropics. Instead they lie in a dry zone of the Pacific and in an area where temperatures are kept low by a cold upwelling of water. Within the larger islands, there are two distinct zones of climate and, hence, of vegetation. The coastal regions and the lowlands are particularly arid. The little rain they do receive quickly disappears through the porous ground, leaving it parched and suitable only for drought-resistant cacti and scrub. The uplands, on the other hand, are high enough to induce precipitation. Mists, known locally as *garúa*, and rain shroud the uplands and allow the growth of tropical forests as dense and lush as any in Amazonia.

Isolated in the ocean, these islands are ideally located for migrant creatures travelling by either air or water. Perhaps the most revered of all is the sperm whale, which can be found in the waters east of Isabela and Fernandina. This giant has been given a number of names, each referring to a particular characteristic. Some derive from its impressive set of teeth. Russians call it *bolshoi plevum* or 'great spouter', for when it exhales after a deep dive, the blow can be 5 metres (16 feet) high and may be heard a kilometre away. Its common English name, sperm whale, comes from the vast reservoir of clear liquid or spermaceti in its bulky head. On cooling, the liquid solidifes into a white wax which, according to early whalers, resembles semen.

Sperm whales are the largest of the toothed whales, their more massive relatives having plates of baleen instead of teeth. There is a marked difference between the sexes. Males are on average 15 metres (50 feet) long and weigh about 45 tonnes, while females are a mere 11 metres (36 feet) long and on average weigh 20 tonnes. The

OVERLEAF: Although a formidable predator, the sperm whale is not aggressive to man unless provoked.

flippers are short and stubby, whereas the tail flukes, used for propulsion, are broad and strong and have a surface area proportionately greater than those of any other whale. The huge head, which takes up one-third of the body length, ends in a blunt, almost square snout above a narrow lower jaw which looks puny in comparison. Yet it is this lower jaw that bears the formidable set of teeth, each weighing 1 kilogram (2.2 pounds). Fifty of these conical teeth are arranged along the lower jaw, while the upper jaw has only tiny vestigial teeth.

The sperm whale's skin is corrugated, giving it a shrivelled prune-like appearance. It is dark grey with blotches of white that increase in size with age, particularly in males. Very old males can be almost entirely white and one such was probably the inspiration behind Moby Dick. Adults often have circular scars on their heads which are the sucker marks of squid, their preferred prey. Squid can be enormous, and scars as wide as 20 centimetres (8 inches) in diameter have been reported, which would come from a squid 45 metres (150 feet) long!

Sperm whales can eat as much as a tonne of squid a day. They forage at all times of day and night, all year round, interspersing their feeding with periods of rest that might last anything between one and eight hours. They tend to prey on deep-water squid, but also feed nearer the surface and may take both fish and jellyfish. Regrettably, damaging and harmful man-made debris such as wire and plastic have also been found in their stomachs.

Around the Galápagos, sperm whales generally feed at a depth of about 400 metres (1300 feet), for that is where squid are found in great number. Elsewhere, though, dives down to 1000 metres (3300 feet) or more are not uncommon and there is evidence to show that sperm whales can dive to over 3000 metres (nearly 10 000 feet). To achieve such depths, they dive at considerable speed, and may stay down for as long as 45 minutes. Their dives are near vertical and they do not appear to swim much at depth for they surface in roughly the same place as they go down. Presumably their strategy is to hover in midwater and ambush squadrons of luminous squid as they swim by. It is during these deep dives that the spermaceti comes in useful. As a whale dives it fills its long nasal passages with water from different depths, which cools some of the liquid spermaceti to wax. The greater the depth, the cooler the water, solidifying more spermaceti and increasing the whale's buoyancy. So the whale can remain in midwater at any depth without having to move to hold position.

On returning to the surface from such a dive, the whale's exhaled breath sounds like an explosion. During a period of feeding, which can last for anything up to 30 hours non-stop, whales will dive again after an interval of only 10 minutes. While in a slow cruising mode sperm wales swim at around 6 km/h (3 knots), but they can reach as much as 40 km/h (22 knots), outpacing most boats. At other times they can be seen resting, possibly sleeping, on the surface in great flotillas, and it is only then that it is sometimes possible to get close to them.

Sperm whales are relatively easy to locate because they emit sounds that can be detected miles away on an underwater sound detector. Getting near them is difficult, though, as they are evasive and staying with a group requires considerable skill. If a boat approaches from the front, they will either dive under it or veer off to the side, and any acceleration frightens them off. So a boat must stay well behind a group until they stop and mill around. Then one has to enter the water very quietly and snorkel over to them, sometimes drifting a long way from the boat in the process.

Females and their calves stay in warm water all year round, living in groups led by an older female. These 20 to 30 strong nursery groups contain pregnant females, and mothers with their suckling calves. Groups may gather together, forming loose harems of up to 80 or so whales. Gestation lasts 14–16 months and the mother then gives birth to a 4 metre (13 foot) long calf while hanging vertically in the water. All the other females in the group surround her during the birth and then nudge the newborn calf to the surface for its first breath of air. The young calf suckles for one to two years, continuing to take its mother's milk well after it has started eating squid. After weaning a calf, the female rests for at least nine months before mating again. She breeds once every 4 to 6 years which means that a harem will usually contain only a few receptive females at any given time.

Males, on the other hand, migrate to and from polar waters. They travel alone rather than in groups, and journey up to tropical waters to breed. In some areas, males fight in order to obtain a short-lived access to the harem. They lock jaws and roll at the surface until the loser backs down and swims away. There appears to be little aggression between males that visit the Galápagos Islands, though, and they move freely between groups of females.

All whales emit sounds and the clicking noises made by sperm whales serve a range of purposes. The sound passes through the head and the spacing of the clicks is proportional to the dimensions of the head. As a result an individual can be identified by its call and members of a group can maintain contact. When the whales are resting, the patterns of clicks are often quite complex and may be being used for more sophisticated communication. During feeding they emit a series of clicks, usually one every second or two, although the clicking rate can increase to 80 clicks per second. The clicks will be reflected back by any object, such as squid, in the path of the sound wave. Listening out for any reflected clicks or echoes helps the whale locate its prey. A captured blind whale was found to be in perfect health with a full stomach, showing the effectiveness of this echolocation system. It is possible that sperm whales also use very loud clicks to stun their prey. This idea was backed up recently when a diver, helping to untangle a sperm whale from a fishing net, was forced to leave the water because the clicks had increased in volume so much that they had become painful.

Killer whales are among the few predators of sperm whales. When a pod of killer whales approaches, the group falls silent and packs tightly together. If the killer whales persist, the sperm whales start clicking again, and keep track of their attackers by increasing the frequency of their clicks and, hence, the accuracy of their echo-location system. Sperm whales always turn to face their attackers because their heads are their least vulnerable part. They will form a circle with their heads facing outwards, if surrounded, or downwards, if the killer whales move underneath them. This is an effective defence against the killer whales and, as a result, they rarely penetrate a group of sperm whales successfully.

Against man, however, this strategy proved disastrous for it made the sperm whales stationary targets. The protective behaviour of the group to calving females was also ruthlessly exploited by whalers who would harpoon each of the surrounding whales in turn. From their discovery in 1712 until recently, sperm whales were the mainstay of the whaling industry. They were taken for the oil in their blubber, the wax in their heads and the ambergris in their gut. The ash-coloured ambergris, once highly valued for use in perfumes, is only produced by sperm whales. A synthetic substance is now used in perfumeries. Ambergris can occasionally be found drifting in the ocean or washed up on the beach. The slaughter reached a peak in 1963 when about 30 000 sperm whales were killed, and it was only in 1984 that the commercial fleets were banned. The populations remaining in each hemisphere are small and largely separate, but in the waters off the Galápagos Islands groups do come together and intermix. Even there, the males form only a small percentage of the population, prompting concern that their numbers may be too low to allow the whales to recover from the slaughter carried out by man through the centuries.

Sperm whales usually inhabit the open ocean and can be seen near the shore only where very deep water is close to land, as in the Galápagos. These islands are the tips of huge underwater volcanoes. Successive eruptions built up the volcanic mountains until their tips rose above the water to form dry land. Just as lava flows

The rope-like formations of *pahoehoe* lava are a stark feature of the Galápagos landscape.

have joined some of the tips to form the island of Isabela, so lava unites the whole archipelago in an underwater platform. This Galápagos Platform is 400 metres (1300 feet) below sea level, while the ocean around it is 2000–3000 metres (6500–10 000 feet) deep. The volcanic mountains appeared above sea level relatively recently, and the oldest islands are thought to be only 3–5 million years old.

The islands are still forming today, for the Galápagos is one of the most active volcanic regions on Earth. Below the Earth's crust is hot molten rock, known as magma. The archipelago lies over a weak point or 'hot spot' in the Earth's crust. There, magma can melt through the crust creating a vent or volcano. Periodically, Magma spills out through the volcano to the surface, and it is then known as lava. Magma containing a lot of trapped gas may erupt through a volcano with tremendous force forming an elegant peak like that of Mount Fuji in Japan. In the Galápagos, the magma usually contains little gas and so flows gently out, solidifying into rounded domes and craters.

The Earth's surface is thought to be divided up into a few rigid plates that move relative to each other. Typically, volcanic activity occurs at the edges of these plates; indeed, 99 per cent of the world's volcanoes are located at plate boundaries. The Galápagos Islands are an exception, for they are sited not on a boundary but on the Nazca plate, which is near to two other plates. These three plates are moving away from each other, and the Nazca plate and, hence, the islands are drifting towards the south-east at some 7 centimetres (2.7 inches) per year. The oldest islands lie in the south-east of the archipelago and have moved about 350 kilometres (220 miles) since their creation. At the same time the youngest islands are still forming over the hot spot in the north-west.

As well as volcanic activity, the area of the Galápagos is subject to earthquakes, subsidence and uplifting. These make the islands unpredictable places to live and those in the north-west are particularly desolate. In some parts, coral reefs have been lifted up, and lie bleached and dead above the ocean surface. The solidified rivers of lava are black and tortuous, pock-marked by the bubbles of gas they contained. Jagged, sienna-coloured rocks and slippery screes of ash litter the slopes. Underwater the scenery is just as dramatic. The more violent eruptions have produced near vertical cliffs. There are vast underwater caverns where shafts of sunlight, penetrating through holes in the roof, lift the gloom and allow glimpses of tunnels beyond. These tunnels, called lava tubes, were left when ancient lava rivers ran dry.

A sustained sign of the turmoil below is the gas issuing from small holes called fumaroles, both underwater and on land. We found an underwater one near Roca

Redonda, a rock jutting up from the sea that marks the very tip of a volcano rising 3000 metres (10 000 feet) from the ocean floor. As we swam towards it in the middle of the ocean, with volcanic islands dotted about and gases bubbling up from some vast magma chamber deep in the bowels of the Earth, it was impossible not to feel apprehensive. Currently volcanic eruptions in this area are few and far between, but the possibility existed, however remote, that one could occur at any minute. The rocks around the hole were covered in an alga peculiar to fumaroles all over the world, and it made the rocks so slimy that we had great difficulty staying upright. The sulphurous gases that issued forth mixed with the water to produce a very dilute sulphuric acid. The divers without bubble helmets soon had tingling lips from the caustic liquid. Even those of us with helmets could smell the sulphur in the small amount of water that seeped past the tight seals. We had taken a thermometer down with us, and stuck it in the sand between the slippery rocks. Although we could feel the warmth of the rocks, we were amazed at what we saw. The temperature reading shot up from 24°C (75°F) to over 50°C (120°F) before we whipped the thermometer away to prevent it shattering.

When the first islands of the archipelago emerged from the sea, some 3–5 million years ago, they were hot rocks totally devoid of life. Yet the wetter parts of the older islands now teem with life. The pioneering species must have been very hardy and adaptable to have journeyed there and established themselves in such a harsh environment. We cannot be certain whence they came or how they got there, but the islands' present-day populations do yield some clues.

The plant and animal groups of the world are not evenly represented on the islands. For example, there are numerous birds there, and many reptiles including the tortoises (*galápagos* in Spanish) from which the islands got their name. But there are no amphibians and very few indigenous mammals. This is because few amphibians or mammals can travel far by sea or air, the only two ways to disperse to an island until people started roaming the world in ships.

Creatures usually need the aid of a current to travel long distances by sea. Numerous currents bathe the Galápagos Islands, flowing from both north and south along the coast of South America, and from the west across the Pacific. The animal life, or fauna, on the islands has more affinity with that of the Panama region than anywhere else, indicating that the south-flowing current played an important part in the colonisation of the Galápagos. The Pacific to the west acts as a barrier, since few plants or animals are able to survive a journey across a vast expanse of ocean. The larvae of marine creatures are probably best adapted for such journeys and some of

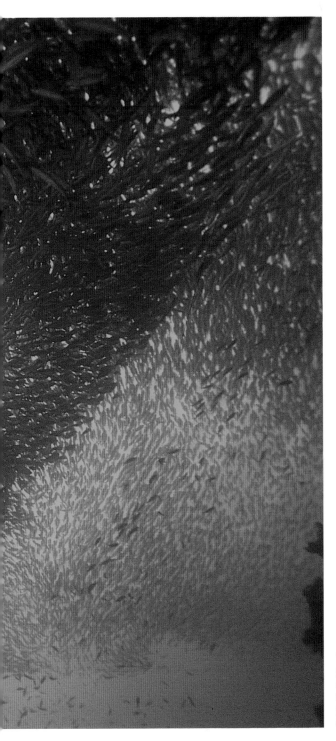

The waters around the Galápagos Islands are highly productive and teem with fish. We encountered this enormous school of brown-striped snappers and, like the sea lions, were enveloped by them. Sea lions are predators of these and other fish, but this sea lion is simply frolicking among his customary prey.

these did reach the Galápagos from Polynesia, probably via the Cocos Islands to the north which intercept the current flowing from the west.

Making use of the currents, agile swimmers such as sea lions, fur seals and penguins would have had little difficulty in reaching the islands. The most famous inhabitants, the giant tortoises, can stay afloat for a considerable length of time and so could have simply been swept there by currents. On the mainland, large chunks of vegetation come loose in the rainy season and may be carried by rivers to the sea. These rafts, some bearing a cargo of animals and their eggs, would take about two weeks to reach the islands from the mainland. Reptiles, with their impermeable skins, are well equipped for such a journey, as are their hard-shelled eggs. Amphibians, on the other hand, need to keep their skin moist with fresh water, so they and their relatively unprotected eggs would perish at sea. Most mammals too would die of heat and thirst if they were afloat for two weeks under the equatorial sun. Many insects and plant seeds would survive the journey by raft, but it is thought that most of the Galápagos's plants arrived by air.

For seabirds, the first islands must have been a welcome new resting place and, in time, a home. Smaller birds and bats also arrived by air, probably with the help of strong winds. Tiny insects, spiders and snails have been found floating high in the atmosphere and some may have been deposited on the islands. Similarly, light plant spores, such as those from mosses, ferns and lichens, are transported long distances by wind. The most important plant transporters of all, though, are birds. They are thought to have carried the seeds of over half the archipelago's plant species in their gut, or stuck to their feet or feathers.

While dispersal across large stretches of ocean is difficult, becoming established in a new area is even more so, and few creatures succeeded. On the Galápagos, the rate of colonisation by plants averages out at one species every 8000–10 000 years. But those that managed to establish themselves on the islands found few competitors there and flourished.

Isolated on their island home, creatures slowly changed as they adapted to their new environment and the opportunities it offered. For example, with few other birds around, insect-eating finches from the mainland had a wide range of new food sources at their disposal on the islands. Gradually the finches developed different-shaped beaks and other adaptations which enabled them to exploit new types of food. Eventually, Darwin's finches were so different from their mainland relatives that they could no longer successfully interbreed with them.

Many of the islands' other inhabitants have also evolved into new and unique species which are only found on the Galápagos Islands and are therefore said to be endemic to them. Much of the archipelago's life is endemic, including the majority of the 28 species of land birds and 5 of the 19 seabirds.

I was particularly fascinated by the endemic flightless cormorant, a mainly black bird with startling bright turquoise eyes. It is the only one of 29 species of cormorant around the world to have lost the ability to fly. With no land predators and plenty of food in the ocean nearby, Galápagos cormorants had no need of flight. They still hold their wings out to dry in the sun, in a posture typical of cormorants worldwide, but their small, ragged wings have lost the keel of the breastbone to which flight muscles were attached. Their streamlined bodies make them adept underwater as they dive for bottom-dwelling fish near the shore. Only with luck can one see them underwater, for they are very wary of predatory sharks and flee from any large shape in the sea. There are a mere 700 to 800 breeding pairs in existence, all concentrated on Isabela and Fernandina on the west side of the archipelago, where their food is most plentiful.

One of the first Europeans to reach the Galápagos, the Bishop of Panama, noted that many of its birds were 'so silly they do not know how to flee'. Living in a haven free from land predators, other animals had also changed in form and behaviour. Their tameness astounded many an early visitor and made the animals very vulnerable to the people who settled on the islands. Few human settlements lasted long but their abandonment did not bring relief. Some of the cattle, horses, goats, pigs, cats, rats and dogs introduced by people into this fragile environment remained and became feral, and their descendants roam the islands to this day. On Isabela, feral dogs are a particular problem. Currently they are restricted to the southern part of the island by an extensive lava field. If and when they cross this barrier, they will certainly eliminate the flightless cormorant from Isabela, leaving Fernandina as its only safe breeding area in the world. People are now attempting to eradicate the dogs in an effort to prevent this catastrophe.

Underwater too, the animals that arrived in the new habitats and colonised them adapted and evolved. Of the 300 or so species of fish found around the Galápagos Islands, nearly a quarter are endemic. We soon came across one of these endemic species, the brown-striped snapper. Individually this is a rather unremarkable fish, being only about 15 centimetres (6 inches) long and coloured silver with dark stripes. But it amazes by its sheer numbers, for it schools in thousands. As we dived in, the wall of fish parted for us, creating a tunnel. They then swam behind us and we were totally enclosed in a sphere of fish. Never before had I seen so many fish or been so completely encompassed by them. As we swam on, they ran in rivers around us.

LEFT: The Galápagos penguin is ungainly on land, but once underwater is fast and surprisingly agile.

RIGHT: Hunted to near extinction for its coat, the Galápagos fur seal is understandably cautious on land.

Such a wealth of life is evidence of the exceptionally high productivity level of the waters around the Galápagos Islands. This is due to the fact that the same system of currents that assisted in their colonisation, particularly the Peru, the South Equatorial and the Cromwell Currents continues to flow around the archipelago. The Peru or Humboldt Current flows up from the south along the west coast of South America, bringing cold water which is rich in nutrients. The South Equatorial Current, fed by the cold Peru Current and by warm water coming down from Central America, flows in a westerly direction through the island chain.

The cold Cromwell Current originates far out in the Pacific and runs in an easterly direction below the surface. Near the equator, winds push water in the northern hemisphere to the right and water in the southern hemisphere to the left. This creates a 'hole' which is filled by water from the Cromwell Current. The upwelling brings with it nutrients from deep within the Pacific Ocean. It is greatest in the west of the archipelago, particularly on the flanks of Fernandina where the coldest and richest waters are to be found.

The nutrients brought by the currents form the basis of food chains upon which many animals of the Galápagos depend. Fish numbers are astronomical, with many species as abundant as the brown-striped snappers. This was very evident on one afternoon dive, when we found ourselves in the middle of what appeared to be fish rush hour. For about an hour, thousands upon thousands of small, red creole fish swam by, seemingly oblivious to anything but their journey. They are said to be the most abundant fish in the Galápagos and we would concur. In stark contrast, the arid lowlands rising up out of the water appear incapable of supporting animals. Yet the teeming life in the coastal margins allows a diversity of animals to inhabit this otherwise barren wasteland, including an estimated 750 000 pairs of breeding seabirds.

The variable currents make navigation difficult and dangerous, and caused early Spanish mariners to christen the archipelago 'Las Encantadas', the Enchanted or Bewitched Islands. We experienced their strength and unpredictability while diving off Wolf, an island in the far north-west. We had to fight our way along an underwater cliff to the tip of the island against currents that seemed to keep changing direction. Even 15 metres (50 feet) down, we were washed back and forth in the swell. When we attempted to swim out towards a pinnacle, we were swept up across the saddle that bridged the gap and thrown against the pinnacle. The current was so strong that when I turned my head sideways to it, my mask started to lift away from my face. Fighting the current, our hands badly cut by barnacles, we struggled for the next 20 minutes or so just to hold position. Eventually we had to let go and were taken out to sea, where we were picked up by our anxious boatman.

The currents vary over the year and changes in them bring seasons which affect the animals and plants of the Galápagos. The Peru Current, driven by the south-east trade winds, dominates from July to December during which there is a cool dry season. When the winds diminish, the South Equatorial Current brings warm water down from the Panama basin and there is a warm, wet season from January to June. Periodically, the trade winds fail and a phenomenon occurs called El Niño. This is Spanish for 'the child', and is named after the infant Christ because, when it happens, it starts soon after Christmas. Instead of the usual prevailing southerly winds, northerly winds blow, driving warm surface water shoreward. The result can be catastrophic. The Galápagos and South America experience torrential rains and floods, while the west Pacific suffers from drought. Even more serious for the archipelago's wildlife is the fact that El Niño can raise the water temperature by as much as 5°C (9°F). The corals and algae, on which many other creatures depend for their food supply, are killed by such high water temperatures. Fish populations crash and as a result many seabirds, sea lions and fur seals die of starvation. Indeed, very few animals escape the effects of El Niño.

The presence of warm and cold water currents has allowed a rather peculiar mix of animals to colonise the Galápagos Islands. Perhaps the most surprising of all is the 35 centimetre (14 inch) tall Galápagos penguin. This little bird is the only penguin found north of the equator and the only one to nest entirely within the tropics. It was almost certainly brought up to the islands with the Peru or Humboldt Current, being descended from the Humboldt penguin which lives along the southern coast of South America.

The penguins only survive in the Galápagos because of the cold Cromwell Current, and they are most commonly seen near the cold upwelling on the north-west side of the archipelago. Even there, they have problems keeping their bodies at the correct temperature. They can spend long periods in cold water, insulated by their thick fat layers and protective feathers. But when they come on to land, they face temperatures that can reach as high as 40°C (104°F) and they have had to develop ways of keeping cool. They hold out their wings to cool in the wind, shade their feet with their bodies, and may pant and hide under overhangs. If none of these measures is sufficient, they will retreat to the water. Their problems are greatest when they moult and lose their protective feathers. During this time they avoid the heat by staying in the shade, and avoid the cold water by fasting.

We found the penguins difficult to get close to in the water. We had to wait for them to swim by, or to creep up on them very, very slowly. Our patience was usually rewarded, though, and they would eventually accept us, if only temporarily. While we snorkelled among them, one dived down and nipped my extended finger. They came within inches of our masks and paddled around or groomed themselves quite contentedly in front of us.

Getting amongst them while they were feeding proved even more difficult. Penguins

OVERLEAF: Everywhere we dived in the Galápagos we were joined by inquisitive sea lions, eager to play.

use their feet as paddles at the surface and as rudders underwater. They 'fly' through the water using their stubby wings. When chasing after a school of fish, they 'porpoise', moving in and out of the water like porpoises, and can reach speeds of 40 km/h (25 mph). So we had to jump into the water a substantial distance ahead of them to watch them feeding. We took a deep breath and waited for them on the bottom behind a shoal of tiny silver fish. Suddenly, the penguins shot through, scattering the bank of fish. The shimmering screen of fish billowed, regrouped, and shattered again and again as the penguins sped round, chasing them in circles, turning somersaults, and darting to and fro.

During the warming of El Niño, such bounty disappears and the penguins face starvation. In 1972 the water temperature rose 5°C (9°F) from the usual 18–22°C (64–72°F). The penguins lost weight, eggs were abandoned and further attempts at breeding failed with a catastrophic effect on their populations. Starvation apart, there are always predators on the prowl. Sharks, fur seals and sea lions all take penguins in the water, and they are now even more at risk on land. Like the flightless cormorant, penguins are sought by introduced animals such as feral dogs, cats and rats. Their defence against land predators is almost pathetic; they turn their backs in the hope that their camouflage against the black lava will suffice.

Another animal that can suffer from overheating is the Galápagos fur seal which, like the penguins, originated in the cold southern waters and almost certainly came north to the Galápagos with the Peru Current. Like its ancestor, the southern fur seal, it has a double-layered coat with long, coarse, outer hairs covering the short, dense fur. The coat is a great insulator in the southern fur seal's subantarctic home, but is not so useful in the Galápagos. In addition, while other southern fur seals spend most of their time in the water, the Galápagos fur seal stays on land in the equatorial sun for as much as a third of the time.

Like the penguins, the Galápagos fur seals tend to concentrate in the islands in the north-west near the cold upwelling and have to use many techniques to keep cool on land. As the day heats up, they hold their flippers against the rocks which are still cool. Heat flows out from the many blood vessels near the surface of the flippers, and the animals cool. By noon it is simply too hot and they must retreat back into the water or move into the shade. In the water, young pups are in danger of being washed away by the swell and so there is competition between females for the shady spots on land.

It is owing to their soft and very thick fur that these seals had nearly become extinct by the early part of this century. Fur seals were slaughtered by the thousands in the nineteenth century, and were only saved because sealing become economically unviable. The population has recovered to between 30 000 and 40 000 individuals, and is now mainly limited by the number of appropriate shady places on the islands. There are about six adult fur seals per 100 square metres (120 square yards) on the Galápagos shores, whereas southern fur seal colonies that do not require shade have population densities ten times as great.

In order to have access to enough females, all requiring shade, a male fur seal on the Galápagos must hold an exceptionally large territory. This presents numerous problems, including the ease with which intruding males can gain access to females before the territory holder can chase them off. More serious is the energy used up in the routine walking and climbing required merely to maintain the area. The males overheat very quickly during such strenuous activity, and their defence of their territory leaves them little or no time to feed. As a result, there is an astonishingly high male mortality rate of 30 per cent per year. Another effect of holding large territories is a smaller difference in size between male and female Galápagos fur seals than in other species of seal. While a small male might find it more difficult to actually acquire a territory he is likely to expend less energy in retaining it than a larger one.

Like many animals in the Galápagos, fur seals are very approachable. We came across some resting in the water, hanging upside down with their hind flippers breaking the surface. We swam carefully towards them so as not to scare them, and quite quickly they accepted our presence. As they lolled in the water, they twisted their heads round in all directions, appearing to have unrestricted movement. They were probably keeping a watch for predatory sharks and killer whales because it is while resting that they are at their most vulnerable. They have large, doleful eyes which seem to belie the boisterous playfulness of the young ones.

Fur seals hunt by night and their huge eyes help them see in the dark. In the evening, before leaving the relative safety of the shallows, they gather in large groups and mill around. Although some are skittish then, this is usually the best time to see large numbers of them underwater. Gradually the groups disperse as they swim out to sea for a night of hunting. They feed on squid and schooling fish, such as anchovies and mackerel, all of which come up towards the surface at night. Unlike many seals they do not dive deep, rarely going down more than 30 metres (100 feet) and are thought never to exceed 100 metres (330 feet) in depth. On nights when the moon is full and bright, visibility underwater improves considerably and the fur seals do not venture out to feed. Their prey tends to remain deep on such nights and the seals themselves are far more vulnerable to shark attacks.

LEFT: Immature male sea lions test their strength in mock battles. This play prepares them for the bloody struggles they enter later in life as they fight over territories and females.
RIGHT: Sea lions nurse their pups for up to a year. The mother leaves her pup in a nursery when she goes to feed at sea. On return, they find each other in the crowded rookery with an exchange of identifying calls.

The fur seals can at first sight be confused with the more boisterous Galápagos sea lions. However, the fur seals look more like bears, having shorter and broader heads, and their ears stick out. The sea lions have smaller eyes and their front flippers are also smaller, which makes them poorer climbers. Consequently, the fur seals prefer to clamber out on to steep rocky coastlines which provide more shade, while the sea lions generally opt for gently sloping beaches. This split in preference helps reduce competition between fur seals and sea lions. Perhaps the main physical difference between the animals, though, is that sea lions have a single-layered coat.

Galápagos sea lions originated in the north, not the south. They are a subspecies of the Californian sea lion, the only noticeable difference being their slightly smaller size. Adapted to warmer climes, they do not have the overheating problems of fur seals and can lie basking in the sun at noon. When wet their coat is dark brown, but after a long laze in the sun it fades to a buff colour. The sexes are easy to tell apart because fully grown males weigh 250–300 kilograms (550–660 pounds), over twice as much as females. They also have very thick necks and a characteristic bump on their forehead.

Sea lions are common throughout the islands, their population totalling around 50 000 individuals at the last count. On land they are rather awkward, getting around by waddling or making galloping jumps, but once in the water their agility is supreme. Using their front flippers for propulsion and their back ones for steering, they shoot through the water twisting and looping as they go. Like the penguins, they will 'porpoise' in and out of the water when swimming fast.

Sea lions do not need such large eyes as fur seals because they hunt during the day, usually in the morning and late afternoon. When a sea lion catches an octopus, it brings the prey to the surface and thrashes it around to stun it before eating. They also eat fish which they kill in the same way, breaking them up at the surface. It is rare to witness a sea lion catching a fish, but we had the good fortune to do so while we were swimming in the vast school of brown-striped snappers. A sea lion shot through the school, creating tunnels as the fish parted and scattered to avoid its jaws. It homed in on one individual, chased it away from the school and cornered it under a rock. Within seconds, the sea lion had grabbed the trapped fish and had swum off to eat it.

With such speed and efficiency in the hunt, it is little wonder that they have so much time to sport. They are notoriously playful and will surf in the waves just for the joy of it. They will pick up and play with sea urchins and pieces of algae, and even marine iguanas are victims of their games. Before we got in the water they had already befriended our inflatable boat. Initially only one or two leapt up on to it, but soon the others caught on and an energetic game of 'king of the castle' ensued. It did not take long for them to find another territory, the dive platform at the back of the boat, and this they contested even with us. Their antics were accompanied by a great deal of barking, splashing and general uproar.

They were just as playful with us underwater, our communication cables providing endless entertainment. Our flippers were tugged and a piece of rope we had taken down proved irresistible to them. They were delightfully mischievous and behaved almost like unruly children, always pushing their luck. They have fantastic acceleration, and feigned attacks by charging straight towards us and turning at the last instant. One particular female, who was easily recognised by a scar on her right flipper, gained such confidence in us that she eventually let us touch her. She rubbed herself against our helmets, and twisted and swirled around us. If we held on to her hind flippers she would turn and give us a playful nip. But otherwise we could hold her, stroke her surprisingly sticky coat, and tickle her. This was our most memorable encounter with sea lions and it was over all too soon.

Sea lions are just as fascinating on land, although in one way not quite as appealing. When we visited a colony or rookery what hit us most forcibly was the smell. While resting on land, sea lions urinate and defecate without moving, and are constantly rolling in their own and other sea lions' excrement. With little rain to wash it away, a dreadful stench rose from the rookery, which took a while to get used to.

Sea lions are segregated into harems, each containing a male and from 5 to 20 females plus pups. The male establishes a territory and then attracts females to it by barking. Sea lions are very social animals, though, and the structure of the harems is loose. The females can move to neighbouring territories with little fuss. They breed almost all year round, with a peak which varies in timing between the different populations around the archipelago. This extended breeding season means that males must fight for a territory throughout the year. They ferociously oppose competition from other males both on land and underwater. Although fights can be avoided by barking and posturing, bloody battles do sometimes ensue. Their clumsiness on land makes gently sloping beaches the most sought-after territory. Unsuccessful and immature males congregate in peaceful groups in less suitable sites, often remote cliffs. But their chance may come, because tenure of territory does not last long. In order to maintain control, the male must stay on guard day and night. Soon he becomes weak from lack of food and is easily ousted by a fresh male. But once fed and strong again, the original male will return to reclaim his territory and females.

A female is most attracted to the male whose territory will best meet a pup's requirements. Ideally the site will have rock pools for the pups to play in and not too much surf that might wash them away. Immediately prior to the birth, the female moves away from the colony to decrease the risk of the pup getting squashed in the crowded rookery. She stays with her newly born pup for four or five days before leaving to feed herself. During that time mother and pup must become familiar with each other's smell and sound. This is crucial because when she comes back from her feeding forays, she has to be able to find the right pup in the mayhem of the rookery. On emerging she gives a greeting call and the pup bleats in response. Their meeting is followed by a period of frantic bleating and nuzzling.

After a month the pup's coat darkens and it joins a nursery guarded by a single female. She restricts the pups to shallow water and pools because of the threat of sharks. If a shark does appear, the parental bull calls an alarm and may enter the water to evict the shark or herd the pups to safety. There have even been reports of a group of males mobbing a shark. Certainly, we found the approach of a big male bull underwater a fearsome sight.

Killer whales live in family groups or pods. They are easily identified by their large dorsal fins; those of the males are tall and straight, unlike the curved fins of the females shown here.

It is when feeding offshore that the sea lion may encounter an even more dangerous predator and one against which they have little defence – the killer whale. These supremely effective predators are often found around the Galápagos and it was there that I had my first encounter with them in the wild. We spotted two males and a female approaching from a distance, which gave us time to jump into the inflatable and start off towards them. We chased them, caught up with them, and managed to stay with them for a while, their sheer size impressing us all.

Male killer whales are slightly larger than females, growing to around 8 metres (26 feet) long and weighing on average 6 tonnes, whereas females are about 7 metres (23 feet) long and weigh 4 tonnes. Both are streamlined and have blunt heads with small beaks and broad, paddle-like flippers. Their most distinctive features, which enabled us to identify them from a distance, are their dorsal fins and coloration. The tall, straight dorsal fin of the male can be up to 2 metres (6.6 feet) high and contrasts with the shorter, curved, more shark-like fin of the female. Their coloration is essentially jet black and white, with glossy black on the back, pure white on the underside and a distinguished white dash over the eye. The only area that interrupts the two-tone effect is a dark grey saddle just behind the dorsal fin. The shape of this saddle, which is not very obvious, and notches on the tail are the only means of recognising individual killer whales.

Staying with killer whales when they are journeying is not easy, for they can swim at 50 km/h (27 knots). They are easy to keep track of, though, because they exhale frequently, producing low, bush-shaped blows. While resting, they dive synchronously and stay underwater for between four and eight minutes, travelling only 150 metres (500 feet) or so per dive. These longer dives are punctuated every now and again with short, shallow dives.

We managed to stay close to them for five minutes or so, before they swam out of range, and at one point we were rather too close. A whale broke the surface just behind and slightly to starboard of the inflatable, seeming near enough to touch. It then went under the boat, and our dread of the whale capsizing the vulnerable inflatable held us breathless until its dark mass appeared on the other side. Our engine was idling, I had my mask ready and I wanted to jump in and join them, but my fear was too great. So I stayed in the boat and accepted, with more than a little regret, the wonder of just being amongst these powerful creatures.

Killer whales usually live as an extended family in groups or pods of between 3 and 25 individuals, the basic social unit being a reproductive female, her offspring and, if still alive, her mother. They are very social whales and have a clearly defined hierarchy within the pod. They are common worldwide, and may inhabit the open ocean where they are free ranging, but they prefer coastlines and colder water. Coastal pods tend to share a large area with other pods, and sometimes combine temporarily to form 'superpods' or clans. Killer whales are found in polar water all year round, their range limited by the ice pack. Unlike other whales living in these extreme conditions, killer whales do not travel to warmer water to breed. Any migration they do undertake is probably prompted by food shortages.

After mating and some 16 months gestation, females give birth to calves about 2 metres (6.6 feet) in length. Young calves of both sexes stay within their mother's pod. This is an unusual arrangement in the animal world for as the calves mature the risk of inbreeding arises. It is thought that the formation of superpods from time to time is a way of encouraging breeding between pods. Within her lifetime, a female killer whale produces five or six calves. She stops breeding at 40 years and lives, on average, for another 10 years or so, whereas the male's average lifespan is only 29 years.

As in other dolphins and whales, sound plays an important part in the lives of killer whales. They use clicks to detect prey in much the same way as sperm whales. They also emit whistles, often used in social situations, and bursts of pulses which sound more like screams. Just as some woodland birds' songs have an underlying melody specific to their wood, so pods of killer whales from a particular area have particular patterns of sounds, and this local dialect is passed down from generation to generation. It probably helps to reduce aggression between neighbouring pods by allowing them to recognise each other quickly. In addition to all these sounds, the noises created by killer whales rising out of the water, breaching or slapping their tails on the surface, are audible for some distance and are another means of communication between them.

Killer whales are at their noisiest when hunting. Their preference for warm-blooded prey is legendary and has given rise to their name. Their diet varies with locality, and it is partly this adaptability which allows them to have such a wide distribution. They have enormous appetites and will take anything from seabirds, sea lions, polar bears, dolphins, seals and rays to the largest animal on Earth, the blue whale. In order to take on such prey, killer whales have to hunt cooperatively and do so to great effect. Using clock-like clicks in murky coastal waters, a pod homes in on its intended victim, and then shares the meat of the unfortunate creature. Those in the Antarctic

OVERLEAF: A vivid splash of colour against the grey lava rock, the Sally Lightfoot crab is named for its habit of skipping across the water or rock pools in search of algae.

cooperate in overturning ice floes to tip off lounging seals. Killer whales frequently raise their heads vertically out of the water to see what is around them, a technique known as 'spy hopping'. This technique is particularly useful for locating land or ice-floe based prey.

Killer whales are more closely related to dolphins than they are to the 'great' whales, and their Latin name, *Delphinus orca*, means 'demon dolphin'. They share many physical dolphin characteristics, including an impressive array of enamelled teeth in both jaws. Small prey are swallowed whole, seals and other medium-sized prey are tossed around to break them up, while very large prey, such as the baleen whales, have to be ripped apart.

Although they are a fearsome sight and have a reputation for being vicious, no killer whale has ever been known to attack a person without provocation. Predictably, this has not been reciprocated. In the past, killer whales were hunted by whaling ships, and they are still slaughtered unnecessarily in some parts of the world because they are thought to compete with commercial fishermen. More peaceable encounters, such as the one we had, are not uncommon off the Galápagos Islands. Unlike dolphins, killer whales rarely take a free ride on the bow wave of a boat. Instead, when a boat approaches, the whales will spy hop, slap the water with their tails as a warning and may breach.

The killer whales and other marine mammals we encountered play an important part in the life of the islands. But for many people it is a reptile, the marine iguana, that epitomises the Galápagos. These animals were made famous by Charles Darwin, who described them less than enthusiastically when he first visited the islands in 1835:

> The rocks on the coast abounded with great black lizards between three and four feet long. . . . It is a hideous-looking creature, of a dirty black colour, stupid and sluggish in its movements.

Marine iguanas line the shores of the islands, and are usually seen sprawled over lava rocks near the sea. At the last count there were estimated to be between 200 000 and 300 000 of them. They are descended from green iguanas of the mainland, which probably floated across on rafts of vegetation borne by the South Equatorial Current. Once on the islands, the iguanas had to adapt to their new home and over generations they slowly changed. Their snouts became blunt so that they could feed on algae, and their forelegs and claws strengthened to cope with feeding in the surf. They also developed the ability to slow their heart rate down during a dive, conserving oxygen and allowing them to spend prolonged periods underwater. Such adaptations enabled these iguanas to become the only truly marine lizards in the world.

The iguanas still spend much of their time on land and seldom venture far out from the shore. So the populations on different islands do not mix and, isolated on their separate volcanic heaps, they have evolved along different lines, resulting in seven distinct types or subspecies. Even those iguanas living on the neighbouring Fernandina and Isabela are different enough to be separate subspecies, and both tend to be larger than their other island relatives.

Marine iguanas range from 60 to 140 centimetres (24 to 55 inches) long. For most of the year they are dull grey to black in colour, but during the breeding season the males develop a red and green tinge down his flanks, the extent of which varies between different subspecies. Their most obvious features are the huge tail, which is longer than the body, and the prominent crest along the back. Also, the head has distinctive pyramid-shaped scales which are used as interlocking devices during head-butting bouts between rival males. Out of the water, marine iguanas look peculiar, ugly to some, but they manage to retain a certain appeal; underwater they appear positively demonic.

Being reptiles, marine iguanas are cold blooded and have to lie in the sun to warm up. Their dark skin both protects them from harmful ultraviolet rays and helps them absorb heat. Their daily activity revolves around maintaining body heat in between bouts of feeding. In the early morning and after feeding underwater, their temperature falls below 25°C (77°F). They then have to bask on the rocks, lying sideways to the sun, to warm up. However, they must also keep their body temperature below 37°C (99°F). Reptiles cannot sweat and, if necessary, will resort to panting to reduce their body heat. When the iguanas get too hot, they turn to face the sun, thereby reducing the surface area exposed to the rays, and stand up to let the wind cool them. They may retreat into cracks in the rock or seek shade during the hottest part of the day.

Dotting the black, wave-washed lava and scuttling over the backs of the seemingly indifferent iguanas, are poppy red crabs. They are called Sally Lightfoot crabs because of their ability to skip across the water, and are also known more prosaically as red lava crabs. The astoundingly bright red of the upperside announces the crabs from some way off and contrasts with the sky blue underside. These audacious colours belie a very wary nature, for the Sally Lightfoots are extremely quick to hide at the

OVERLEAF: Found only in the Galapagos, the marine iguana feeds underwater on carpets of marine algae.

slightest movement. A serious threat will elicit two jets of water shot out in defence. Underwater, they fall prey to moray eels and hawkfish, and on the shore, to the patrolling herons. The marine iguanas pose little threat, though, while they lie basking in the sun.

Bright green and dull red sea lettuce-type algae are the iguana's preferred foods, but they will also eat other algae, small crabs and any flesh that comes their way such as the afterbirth of sea lions. Their blunt snouts enable them to graze on close-cropped algae, and their three-pointed or tricuspid teeth provide a good cutting edge. Algae do not grow well on steep rocks shaded for much of the day, and are most luxuriant on south-facing shorelines with a gentle gradient. So these are the areas iguanas favour, particularly those exposed at low tide. If they have to, male iguanas will dive to feed during the middle of the day when they have warmed up sufficiently. The young iguanas and the smaller females probably have too small a body mass to be able to keep warm in the cold water.

All reptiles move sluggishly when cold, but even when warm marine iguanas are never particularly fast. They crawl on land, and underwater they swim using serpentine undulations of their broad tail and body, with their legs tucked in. They hold their heads high in the water, rather like a child learning to swim, but seem unconcerned when large waves crash over them. Typically, an iguana will stay under for just a few minutes during a dive. Larger males will dive down to 15 metres (50 feet) in search of algae and can stay under for up to half an hour. They use their long claws to cling on to the rock while browsing and can hold position even in very rough conditions.

Marine iguanas can lose as much as 10°C (18°F) in body temperature during a dive. Even when low tide occurs during midday, allowing them to browse on exposed algae, they still get cold in the surf. On emerging they lie out in the sun again, and snort. The sight of a group of marine iguanas snorting is rather absurd, but it is an essential activity. They take in a lot of salt with their food and must excrete the excess. Extremely efficient salt glands just above the eyes produce a concentrated fluid that passes down a duct to the nostrils, and is shot out from the nose. As the day draws to a close, they catch the last rays of the sun gathered together in large groups to conserve body heat through the night.

Stoic on land, marine iguanas are timid underwater. While we were with them, very few attempted to come into the water to feed and it took a great deal of patience to get close to them. If we approached them before they had dived, they would beat a hasty retreat back to land. So we waited in shallow water being buffeted by a swell that built up and delivered a set of big waves every ten minutes or so. When we spotted an iguana moving down the rock, we would watch as it entered the water and started swimming along the surface. With waves crashing over both us and the iguana, we would try to keep it in sight until it dived. Then we would snorkel to the spot as fast as possible and hope to locate it, helped by the fact that, once underwater, iguanas do not swim any great distance. But even when we got close to one scrabbling about on the bottom, a swell would invariably pick us up and move us on to or past the iguana, which would immediately head off back to land. The sea lions, lovable as they are most of the time, also proved a nuisance. To our great frustration, they harassed the iguanas by pulling their tails and frightened off the few we managed to get close to.

Charles Darwin also noted the timidity of iguanas in the water:

> I several times caught this same lizard, by driving it down to a point, and though possessed of such perfect powers of diving and swimming, nothing would induce it to enter the water; and as often as I threw it in, it returned in the manner above described. Perhaps this singular piece of apparent stupidity may be accounted for by the circumstance, that this reptile has no enemy whatever on shore, whereas at sea it must often fall a prey to the numerous sharks. Hence, probably, urged by a fixed and hereditary instinct that the shore is its place of safety, whatever the emergency may be, it there takes refuge.

In the water, sharks are a threat to young and adult iguanas alike. On land the young are vulnerable to capture by Galápagos hawks, great blue herons, lava herons and snakes, and the iguanas' eggs, buried in the sand, are eaten by mockingbirds and snakes. But during their period of evolution on the Galápagos, there were no land predators that posed a threat to adult iguanas. As a result, they feel more secure on land than they do in the water and the adults still stand their ground rather than retreat when danger looms there.

Iguana numbers were originally limited by the availability of exposed rocky coasts, where algae grow prolifically, and the number of nesting sites for females. Then people came, bringing dogs, cats and other predators. Today, feral dogs living along the coasts may consume more than 15 per cent of a colony. To compound the problem, it is the larger, sexually mature iguanas that tend to stand their ground and so get eaten.

They also suffer periodically from El Niño. In 1982–3 there was a 'super' El Niño

LEFT: A barberfish; so named for its habit of cleaning other fish.

RIGHT: As the juvenile king angelfish matures its colours will darken.

during which their favourite types of algae died, the sea level rose dramatically and consistent heavy swells made feeding difficult. As much as 65 per cent of some populations died and, as with seabirds and marine mammals, breeding attempts ended in almost total failure. This El Niño also had a terrible effect on many other animals, including the corals that grow in some parts of the Galápagos Islands.

Of all the wonders this archipelago affords, perhaps the greatest is the opportunity to see penguins one day and corals the next. Corals require warm water to grow and

away from the cold upwelling in the west, the water is just warm enough for them, particularly around Floreana. But corals cannot tolerate changes in water temperature of more than a few degrees. In 1982–3, the water reached a particularly high temperature and remained high for an unusually long time. As a result, 90 per cent of the corals in the Galápagos died. Corals grow very slowly and it may be decades before the rocks have live coral scattered over them once again.

Around the coral, and more widely dispersed over the archipelago, are a few typical coral reef fish. Most families of tropical fish are represented in the Galápagos, if only by one or two species. For example, the angelfish are represented by the king angelfish, which reaches 25 centimetres (10 inches) or so in length. This beautiful fish, almost rectangular from the side, is dark blue to black with a white bar running down each flank and a brilliant yellow tail. It eats mainly sponges, microscopic plants and animals in the water called plankton, and algae. Since all of these are affected by El Niño, the king angelfish were decimated in 1982–3.

There are also three species of the small, colourful butterflyfish so popular among aquarium-keepers. One that we saw quite regularly is called locally the barberfish, presumably because of its habit of grooming or cleaning other fish. On a tropical coral reef, a cleaner wrasse or cleaner goby does this job, but in the Galápagos the barberfish has filled the niche. When we saw this 15 centimetre (6 inch) long, yellow and black fish, it was usually surrounded by other species of fish, all patiently queueing for its attentions. The barberfish removes old scales, mucus and parasites from its customers, doing them a valuable service whilst gaining food for itself.

These productive waters are home to innumerable other fish common to tropical coral reefs, including parrotfish, damselfish, goatfish, snappers, grunts, groupers, surgeonfish, triggerfish and huge schools of silvery jacks. Associated with them are, of course, the big predators – the sharks. We had our most impressive encounter with sharks in the Galápagos while we were up in the far north on Wolf, a very exposed island absolutely covered in seabirds. We approached the windward side of the island in the inflatable and, in between battling against the rather large waves, had a look over the side. To our amazement, the seabed seemed to be moving. We quickly tumbled into the water and found that the moving bottom was, in fact, a huge school of about 80 hammerhead sharks.

At first, we were surrounded by hammerheads. They reach over 4 metres (13 feet) in length and are said to be unpredictable. Perhaps naively, I felt secure in the knowledge that I had company in the water and relaxed. Groups of hammerheads are usually difficult to get close to unless you hold your breath, which will bring them in a little but obviously cannot last for long. Yet here we had them below us, among the boulders behind, out to sea in front and always emerging out of the blue haze on either side of us. After a while, the school shifted and swam by in formation a number of times, clearly silhouetted against the sunlit surface. In between their cruises, they stopped and milled round. We tried swimming out towards them, but they just moved away, keeping their distance. Individual hammerheads behave very differently. They are generally much more inquisitive and often frighten divers by coming up to them unexpectedly from behind. Some members of this group were very curious and swam within 3 metres (10 feet) of us, their large black eyes holding us in a steady gaze. Most continued to stay well back, though, frustrating our efforts to get close, and eventually they cruised into the distance, not to return.

Viewed from any angle, hammerheads are bizarre, almost alien looking creatures. Their name comes from the wide, flattened, almost rectangular head that projects out from the body rather like the head of a hammer. The circular eyes are widely separated, being at either end of the head. There are nine species of hammerhead shark altogether and the ones we swam among were scalloped hammerheads. These sharks are so-called because the front edge of the head is faintly scalloped, a detail that is hard to pick out unless you are close.

The oddly shaped head may help the manœuvrability of the hammer-heads in the water by acting as a wing. It may also increase the shark's sensory powers. Hammerheads feed on fish, rays, other sharks, squid, octopuses and crustaceans. Like all sharks, they can locate their food by detecting the weak electric fields generated by the muscles of their prey. The fields are detected by electroreceptors in pits concentrated around the head. Since the hammerhead has a wide, flattened head, its electroreceptors are spread across a wider area than other sharks, and this may increase its field of 'view'. Such a wide search device would be of particular advantage when feeding on prey that hide in sand, such as rays.

Hammerheads occur worldwide in warm-temperate and tropical seas. They live in coastal and offshore waters rather than in the middle of the ocean, and range from the surface down to 300 metres (1000 feet). Young hammerheads can often be found in the shallow bays in which they are born.

Females usually come inshore to give birth to 30 or so young. These have developed within the mother, each sustained at first by a yolk sac. This later developed into a

OVERLEAF: Time spent getting close to a school of hammerhead sharks is never wasted; they are a particularly remarkable sight when seen in silhouette against the sunlit surface of the sea.

placenta which attached to the uterus, and all the nutrients the embryo needed passed from the mother through the placenta. The pups are 40–50 centimetres (16–20 inches) long at birth and, although fully formed and independent, are very vulnerable to predation. Other species of shark will eat them and cannibalism is rife. Adult male hammerheads caught near pupping grounds have been found to have a high proportion of young hammerheads in their stomachs. The young sharks feed on fish and crustaceans found on nearby reefs. They grow fast at first, but their growth rate slows to 10 centimetres (4 inches) per year as they get older. Males are thought to mature when they are 10 years old, and females when they are 15 years old and about 2.5 metres (8 feet) long. This late maturation, together with the heavy predation on young ones, means that large litters are necessary in order to maintain the populations.

The sexes are easily told apart by the paired claspers found in the genital region of males, which females lack. Many of the females we saw bore scars. Some of these may have been a result of mating, for the male induces the female to copulate by biting her, but immature females were also scarred. Although aggression within a species of shark is rare, scalloped hammerheads within a school can get quite vicious with each other. Generally, the schools are made up largely of females, with just a few males. Females within a school seem to prefer the central position and will swim into and hit one another to gain that place, so becoming scarred. In schools of smaller fish, the purpose of being in the centre is to decrease the individual fish's chances of being eaten by a predator. This cannot be the case in hammerhead schools because these sharks are top predators. It is possible that the dominant females – those that secure the prime places within a school – gain some advantage in access to males during the breeding season.

No one is even sure why hammerheads school, but there are several possible benefits of this behaviour. Scalloped hammerheads typically school during the day when they are not feeding. The schools tend to form near the edge of a steep reef face or at a pinnacle in open water. At dusk they leave singly or in small groups to forage in deeper water and return at dawn to cruise the same site. By swimming slowly all day, rather than wandering long distances into unfamiliar territory, they save energy. They remain in a known area, in which the hunting grounds are familiar. They have easy access to the opposite sex for mating. Also, the 'home' or central resting place may serve as a good reference point when hunting in the dark.

There are a number of other species of shark that usually frequent these waters, many of them familiar inhabitants of reefs throughout the Pacific and, indeed, the world. We saw a few small whitetip reef sharks, inquisitive but unaggressive animals that live close to the reef. But apart from these and the hammerheads, we found a surprising paucity of sharks overall. We then learnt that in 1989, Japanese trawlers slaughtered an estimated 40 000 sharks. They cut off just the fins, to be made into shark-fin soup, and threw overboard the carcasses, which were swept inland and piled up on the beaches. Some species seemed in imminent danger of local extinction and, although pressure from conservationists seems to have halted the destruction, the future holds no guarantees. This is yet another sign that, unless we curb our activities in the Galápagos, we are in danger of losing the unique assemblage of life in this fragile wilderness.

THE CALIFORNIAN KELP FOREST

Of green days in forests and blue days at sea.
Robert Louis Stevenson.

Many people imagine that California's coast is a surfer's and sunlover's paradise with golden beaches, warm seas, slow rolling waves and an ever present sun. In the south near San Diego, it is not unlike this, but much of California's coast is the rocky edge of the North American plate. Cliffs, caves and coves are gently eroded by the Pacific swell or, on rough days, pounded by huge Pacific rollers. The result is a very beautiful coast and, just as important, an unusual and fascinating underwater habitat.

Although we knew that the water would not be warm, our first dive off Monterey came as a shock. Even wearing a thick wet suit, the chill quickly penetrated. The temperature of the water is partly due to a deep canyon running along the coastline. Cold water from deep down in the canyon wells up and is joined by a cold current flowing from the north, known as the California Current.

During the summer months a huge bank of fog moves back and forth across the coastline. Some days it drifts several miles inland, enveloping everything in damp mist, and the next it may hang out at sea. These Californian fogbound summer days are the result of the warm moisture

The Channel Islands off southern California are surrounded by cold, clear water – ideal conditions for the growth of luxuriant kelp forests.

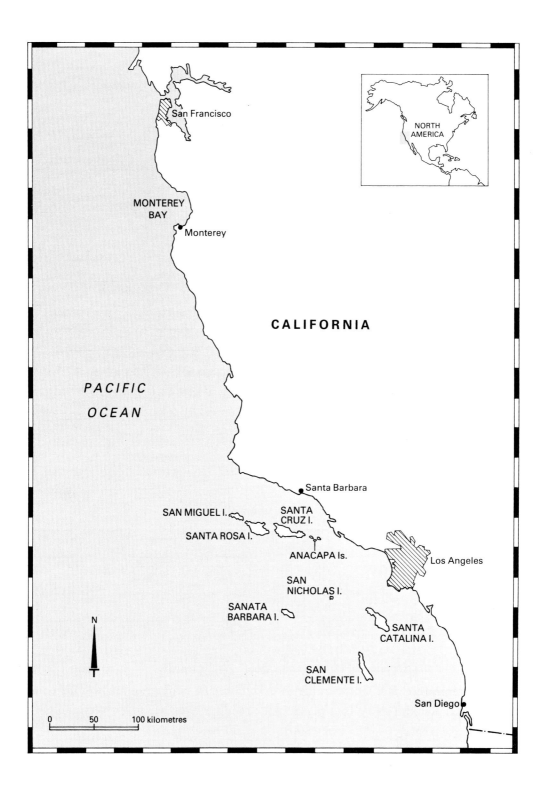

San Francisco

MONTEREY
BAY

Monterey

CALIFORNIA

PACIFIC

OCEAN

NORTH
AMERICA

Santa Barbara

SAN MIGUEL I.

SANTA
CRUZ I.

SANTA ROSA I.

ANACAPA Is.

Los Angeles

SAN
NICHOLAS I.

SANATA
BARBARA I.

SANTA
CATALINA I.

N

SAN
CLEMENTE I.

San Diego

0   50   100 kilometres

laden air blowing in from the Pacific meeting the cold water of the California Current. The sudden cooling of the warm air causes either precipitation or fog. On a good day, when there is no onshore breeze, the sun's heat swiftly clears away the fog, leaving the air clean and fresh.

Thriving in the cold water is an extraordinary abundance of plant and animal life, for this water is laden with nutrients. Like any marine habitat, the richer the water is in nutrients, the more life it supports – and life comes in all sizes. Californian waters are home to a myriad of creatures from the giants of the oceans, the blue whales, to millions of microscopic animals and plants. Most importantly, from our point of view, the rock that forms the beautiful cliffs also provides a permanent and stable seabed on which giant kelp can anchor itself.

Giant kelp belongs to a group of plants called algae. Algae live in wet places, be it in soil, in snow, in streams or in the sea. Algae range in size from plants invisible to the human eye to the giant kelp that can reach 60 metres (200 feet) in length. In the sea, the tiniest algae are the phytoplankton which drift in surface waters, while others such as kelp are permanently anchored. Those which we can see without the aid of a microscope are commonly called seaweeds. They include marine grasses, and various red, green and brown algae. Brown algae or kelps are the largest and fastest growing seaweeds. Of the twenty or so species of brown algae in California, giant kelp is the biggest. It grows best at depths of between 8–20 metres (25–65 feet), where it can form thick forests.

We were told that the kelp beds of California would look like marine versions of the state's Giant Redwood forests, and indeed they do. They look like forests, feel like forests and literally behave like forests but, instead of squirrels, jays and deer, there are bright orange fish, bat rays, sea lions and seals. There are also cyclical changes, although the seasons within the water differ slightly from those on land.

In March, winds start to blow that deflect the cool Californian Current westwards, and water wells up from deep within the Pacific Ocean to replace it. This upwelling water contains the marine equivalent of compost, the decomposed remains of millions of sea creatures of all varieties that have died and sunk to the bottom of the ocean. These nutrients, combined with the summer sunlight, provide the ingredients for the marine plants to make their food. With such a wealth of nutrients the phytoplankton feed and reproduce rapidly, resulting in extraordinary population explosions commonly called plankton blooms. These provide food for countless microscopic animals

OVERLEAF: On their northward migration, grey whales feed in the forests, sieving small crustaceans from among the kelp.

and reduce the visibility in the water drastically. While a plankton bloom lowers the amount of light penetrating to the kelp plant and therefore inhibits growth, the kelp also thrives on the nutrients and its growth outlasts the short-lived blooms. At this time of year the kelp prospers and can grow at a staggering 60 centimetres (24 inches) per day, making it the fastest growing plant on Earth.

In September and October, the north-westerly winds die down and the cold upwelling ceases. The oceanic water that starts washing the coast at this time contains relatively few nutrients and the phytoplankton populations shrink. The water then becomes clear, making this the best time of year to dive. The kelp growth is also arrested, although the remaining summer's growth is still very lush.

From November to February, the cool-loving kelp slowly decays as a warmer current, the Davidson Current, flows up from the south. In El Niño years the kelp decays more quickly, possibly due simply to the higher water temperatures or also to the dearth of nutrients typical of warmer water. The kelp's deterioration during the winter may be accelerated by storms originating in the Pacific to the west or ocean swells from the north. Because water is much heavier than air, the force of a storm swell can be over 50 times greater than that of a wind travelling at the same speed. Battered by the waves, the kelp forests are torn to shreds and countless animals are washed away with the debris. Often the kelp only loses its leafy parts, as many trees do, and the plant itself will regenerate in the spring and can live for seven years or more. In very severe storms, however, kelp plants may be torn from the seabed and great tracts of forest destroyed.

To flourish, kelp needs rock to anchor to, currents to replenish nutrients in the water, sunlight and cool water. It is not only California that provides these conditions. In the southern hemisphere, Argentina, Chile, South Africa, Australia and New Zealand are all graced by these fabulous underwater forests. In the northern hemisphere, the plants grow along the Pacific coast of America, from Mexico all the way to Alaska. Along that western seaboard the best place to see them is around the Channel Islands off southern California. These are a group of eight major volcanic islands off the coast between Santa Barbara and San Diego.

We travelled down from Monterey to the Channel Islands on a similar route to the one which grey whales would take in a few months' time. These animals spend their summer feeding in the rich waters of the Arctic Ocean and Bering Sea. They obtain most of their food by stirring up the seabed with their snouts, sucking in silt

Divers never tire of the beauty of kelp and the profusion of life found there.

and sand and then filtering out tiny animals, using the 300 or so baleen plates that project down from the upper jaw. When winter approaches and the pack ice begins to cover the bays, they journey southwards to their mating and calving areas off the peninsula of Baja California in Mexico. Each leg of the journey can be as much as 10 000 kilometres (6200 miles) and takes them several months. During the southward migration and the subsequent months of breeding, they are thought to fast.

Unlike other whales, grey whales stay in shallow water, sometimes in the surf. They provide a wonderful spectacle as they pass along the Californian coast in November and December, a mere 2 kilometres (1.2 miles) from the shore. On their return journey they may stray even closer and enter the kelp forests, often being seen only 200–400 metres (650–1300 feet) from shore. They may do this partly to hide their recently born calves from predatory killer whales, for they will retreat into the kelp at the first sign of an attack. Grey whales break their fast on this northward migration and so also enter the forests to feed. They scoop great mouthfuls of kelp, possibly to strain it for the numerous small crustaceans living near the kelp and on the surface of the blades.

On our arrival at the Channel Islands, we were relieved to find that the water was crystal clear. The top of Anacapa, one of the northernmost islands, yielded an excellent view of the archipelago. A broken line of volcanic islands ranging in size from several kilometres to just a few metres long stretched into the distance. Sheer cliffs rose above a green crystal sea, bordered by golden kelp, with blue water beyond and a light blue sky framing the whole scene.

The real magic, though, lay underwater. Beneath the canopy of the kelp was a breathtaking arena illuminated by shafts of sunlight. To visualise what diving in giant kelp is like, imagine you are an owl swooping through the branches of an open wood; you can discern colours and creatures on the ground and fly down to investigate and shelter in the top branches. In the same way, we as divers could explore the entire height of the forest, from its hidden, ground-dwelling anemones to the bird-like fish sheltering in the canopy.

The key creature in this maze of interdependent life is the kelp. Unlike land plants, kelp does not need to draw nutrients up from the ground through root and stem to the leaves. The leaf-like blades of the kelp can absorb nutrients directly from the water. But kelp does need to anchor itself to a rock and this is done by the holdfast. Root-like projections, known as haptera, grow out from the base of the kelp plant to form the holdfast. When the haptera reach a firm base they glue themselves firmly on to it. The glue is exceedingly strong, perhaps one of the strongest in nature, for it must hold the giant, buoyant plant in place when huge swells and storms pull against it. Darwin found the tenacity of kelp remarkable: 'I know few things more surprising than to see this plant growing and flourishing amidst those breakers of the western ocean, which no mass of rock, let it be ever so hard, can long resist.'

As the kelp plant grows, new outer haptera anchor it and the original pioneers in the centre of the pile gradually get eaten or die, creating gaps in the holdfast. Any tiny hole can provide a valuable home for colonists, and the holdfasts are inhabited by countless microscopic, as well as larger, animals. Brittlestars, snails, crabs, tiny urchins, worms and many other creatures quietly gnaw away at the holdfast. If the growth of its haptera does not keep up, the kelp gradually loses its grip and is eventually wrenched from the rock and set adrift.

For the tiny young plants that begin to grow on a small pebble or stone instead of the real rocky seabed, the future is bleak. At first there is no discernible difference and the small plant proudly grows up towards the surface, which can be as much as 30 metres (100 feet) above. But as the plant increases in length it is buffeted more and more by currents, waves and surges. The little pebble is no longer heavy enough to hold the plant in place and it is bounced through the kelp forest. It finally ends up with the drift kelp – pieces of kelp that have broken off, fallen to the forest floor and drift along with currents and tides.

Growing from the holdfast are long vine-like structures called fronds, twisting around each other as they make their way up to the light. Fronds are made up of stipes and blades, which are the equivalent of a land plant's stems and leaves. At the top of each frond there is usually a small gas-filled float or bladder. This provides buoyancy, holding the blades borne on the stipes up to the surface and sunlight. The stipes and blades need to be tough and very flexible to allow them to withstand the pull of surges and currents, and the turbulence of waves. They are also covered by a mucous layer to make them slippery. This helps to prevent animals getting a purchase on the plant, either to colonise it or eat it. Over time, though, the blades do get eaten, animals set up home on them and they get battered in the waves. So they need to be continually replaced. New fresh growth starts at the base of an old kelp blade, and as it extends and gradually becomes the bulk of the blade, the ragged bits fall off and join the drift kelp.

The blades are vital for the growth of the kelp because they are the food factory. Kelp blades are wrinkled like seersucker cotton to increase the surface area through which they can absorb water, nutrients and carbon dioxide from the sea. The blades

LEFT: Gas bladders lift young kelp blades towards the sunlight.

RIGHT: The splendid Norris's top shell carries feeding barnacles.

combine these substances to synthesise or produce food, using sunlight as the source of energy. So the process is called light synthesis or photosynthesis. Almost the entire plant is able to photosynthesise, but 90 per cent of the sunlight essential for the process is filtered out by the upper blades or canopy. So these blades have to carry the responsibility of producing virtually all the food.

The stipe acts as a channel along which food made in the blades passes to all the other parts of the plant. It is this ability to move food around that gives kelp an advantage over most other marine algae. It allows growth to continue at an extraordinary rate so that the kelp soon towers above the seabed, cutting out light to smaller plants.

Without giant kelp, the only surfaces available to marine life would be those on smaller plants and the rocks and sand of the seabed. The kelp plant increases the surface area available to marine creatures for resting, shelter and feeding, by about fifteen times. A wealth of plant and animal life takes advantage of this and throughout the year the kelp is home to many creatures. Some eat it, some live on it, some shelter in it, some hunt in it and some, like the grey whale, are merely visitors.

The animals that graze the living kelp include snails, abalone, some small crustaceans and fish. One of the prettier little grazers is a snail with a brownish shell and a bright orange foot called Norris's top shell. Snails scrape at their food using a ribbon-like structure covered in minute teeth known as a radula. Norris's top shell scrapes away at the surface layer of the kelp in a methodical, apparently unstoppable way. It starts off on the holdfast at the bottom of the plant, and grazes its way along the length of the plant. Once up in the canopy, it eats along to the end of a blade and drops off, tumbling to the seabed. If it manages to find another kelp plant before it is eaten by some hungry rock crab, up it goes again. Many do get eaten and so their numbers never become large enough to seriously affect the kelp.

Fourteen other snails also eat kelp but, fortunately for the plant, its defences keep their impact to a minimum. The kelp's mucous layer makes the young blades difficult for these grazers to manage. Older fronds gradually lose this protective sheath and it is mainly these which are attacked, and sometimes destroyed, by the snails. Thin films of algae start to grow over the old fronds providing a nourishing starter for the snails before they get down to the kelp itself.

When young sea stars settle out of the plankton, they make their home at the base of the blades and eat the kelp. This is only a temporary home, though, and they soon migrate down to the seabed where they spend their adult days. A number of small crabs, and isopods and amphipods (tiny shrimp-like creatures) feed on living kelp, but their effect is small because their numbers are kept in check by the numerous fish that eat them. More serious for the kelp blades are the grazing fish, such as halfmoons or Catalina perch and opaleyes.

Halfmoons are so-called because they are dark blue on the top of their bodies with a lighter underside. They are not restricted to kelp forests and are commonly found on rocky reefs all along the coast. In the kelp, they form large schools and move from plant to plant in feeding forays. Their diet also includes other algae and animals that live on the seabed, such as bryozoans and sponges. It is only when these alternative foods are in short supply that the halfmoons may seriously damage the kelp, totally stripping plants of their blades. However, larger fish such as sand bass and rockfish find halfmoons a tasty meal, as do seals and sea lions. The canopy of the kelp forest provides them with shelter from these predators, as well as providing them with food.

Opaleyes are usually about 30 centimetres (1 foot) long but can reach double this length. They have a grey-green body with a characteristic white spot on each side and, as their name implies, opal-like blue eyes. Like halfmoons, they flit around the forests in schools but concentrate much more on kelp and other algae. Opaleyes have developed a very effective method of nipping bits off the tough kelp blades. They bite and hang on with their teeth while twisting their body from side to side until the mouthful of kelp breaks free, leaving a characteristic circular hole in the blade.

Apart from these animals, relatively few depend on the fantastic resource of living kelp for their food. This demonstrates the success of the plant's defences. In common with most of the world's animals and plants, though, kelp cannot prevent harvesting by man, and it has been gathered since 1910. Originally it was used in the production of potash and, since this is an ingredient of gunpowder, the kelp harvesting industry flourished during the First World War. More recently, the industry has boomed again because of demand for a substance in kelp called algin. Algin is used, among other things, as an emulsifier, a gelling agent and a stabiliser. It ends up in over 70 industrial and household products including beer, toothpaste, paint, ice-cream and sweets.

The kelp harvesting industry is concentrated in California where machines like marine lawn-mowers plough through the kelp beds, cutting off the surface canopy and collecting it on conveyer belts. Only the top metre or so of the plant is taken, and the rest remains unharmed and continues to grow. Fortunately, there appears to be no significant change in the animal populations of harvested kelp forests. So long as the marine farmers adjust their rate of harvesting to suit the kelp's growth season and growth rate, an equilibrium is maintained and the kelp forests continue to thrive.

There are many factors that can adversely affect the kelp's growth rate and, hence, the harvest. These include high water temperatures, grazing sea urchins and pollutants. The damage may be widespread, such as that caused by El Niño, or localised, such as around industrial outflows. Sewage, in particular, can damage the kelp in two ways. It clouds the water, decreasing the amount of light penetrating to the plants and so reducing photosynthesis, and the kelp plants start to decline. More seriously, sewage contains large quantities of nutrients that seem to attract certain species of sea urchins. These urchins, short of food due to the gradual decline of the kelp plants, feed on the young kelp fronds and prevent them from growing to maturity. Like garden plants, kelp also suffers from diseases. One infection called black rot eats its way into the blades, spreads very easily and causes massive loss of kelp.

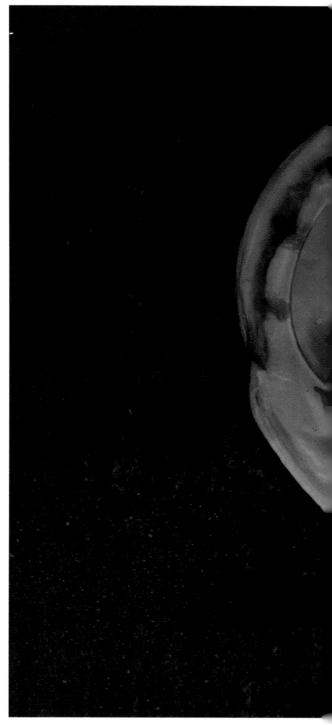

The iridescent inside of an abalone shell. The over-collection of this mollusc for its meat is depriving the forest of this beauty. The shell is also popular as jewellery.

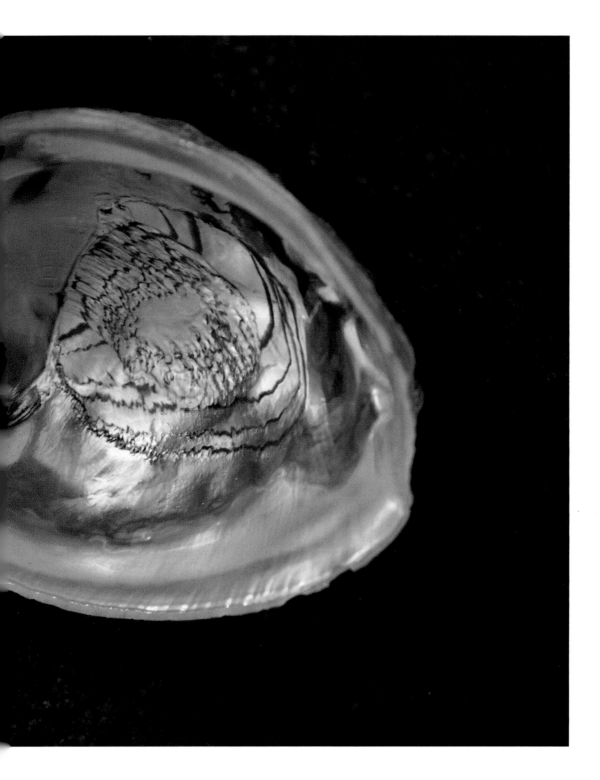

Storm surge, waves and the activities of the forest's other inhabitants also take their toll on the kelp, producing a rain of scraps and bits of kelp that litters the seabed. Many of the animals living there take advantage of this wonderful supply of food. Among the drift-kelp eaters are crustaceans (including lobsters), starfish, sea urchins and abalone. Abalone are single-shelled molluscs, resembling giant limpets that have been squashed. There are a number of species in various shapes, sizes and colours, but all are difficult to find, being well camouflaged on the rocky reef. Rather like the kelp holdfast, an abalone shell will often be a microcosm in its own right. It can be host to all sorts of smaller creatures, including barnacles, hydroids (sea firs), corals, sponges and tiny algae.

Abalone are among the more famous kelp forest inhabitants because they are considered to be a delicacy by many people. These molluscs tend to stay in one place, waiting for bits of kelp to drift by. When they move they become vulnerable, but while stationary they can hold themselves on to a rock with incredible force. To lever them off the rock divers use a pry bar, known locally as an ab bar. This needs to be designed and used carefully because abalone are haemophiliacs, which means that when they are cut, their blood does not clot and they bleed to death. Due to mounting concern about the severe decrease in abalone populations, the ab bar must by law have smooth edges to reduce the chances of cutting and, hence, killing an abalone during an unsuccessful attempt to prise it from a rock. However, despite the concern, too many divers have collected and continue to collect abalone, with a peak of 1.5 million having been gathered in 1957. Since then, a dearth of the preferred pink and red abalones has forced divers to shift to the less desirable black variety, seriously depleting their numbers as well. Now there are some protected areas where abalone only have to contend with their natural predators. However, there is another recent development which may help to restore the balance and reduce the damage to abalone; aquaculture. Marine farmers are rearing abalone and feeding them on specially grown kelp as well as kelp harvested by the marine lawn-mowers, so relieving some of the pressure on natural abalone populations.

Other drift-kelp eaters, the red and the purple sea urchins, move around a little more than abalone, but not much. In a healthy kelp forest with a well-balanced community, urchins do a useful job of clearing away debris. Their populations are kept in check by predators, particularly sea otters, sheephead wrasse, starfish and lobsters. But from time to time, favourable conditions or reductions in the number of predators allow an unusually large proportion of young urchins to survive. Then sea urchin populations explode, and may reach densities of up to 300 urchins per square metre (nearly 30 per square foot). No kelp forest can provide enough debris to feed such a crowd. In an area damaged by storms or where kelp growth is poor, even an average density of urchins will rapidly exhaust the stock of drift kelp. Whatever the cause, when the drift kelp supply runs low there is a dramatic change in urchin feeding behaviour.

Hungry sea urchins move to find food and shift their diet from one comprised largely of drift kelp to one of living kelp. As they slowly make their way along the seabed, it is the holdfasts they reach first. They graze away at this easily accessible food with devastating effects. Soon the kelp plant is sheared off at seabed level and set adrift. An army of sea urchins, for that is what they look like, can totally destroy an area of kelp forest in a matter of weeks. The resultant wasteland is termed an urchin barren and, until most of the urchins die off or move on, any new kelp plant that tries to establish itself will get eaten. Such a huge number of urchins produce countless larvae and, if many of these survive the plankton stage and are not later wiped out by disease, the problem continues.

Several decades ago, the Californian kelp forests were ravaged by sea urchins. These infestations may form part of a natural cycle. Alternatively, they may have been provoked, at least partly, by pollution and by overhunting of urchin predators such as sheephead wrasse, lobsters and sea otters. By 1960 the urchins had had such an impact that there were very few areas of kelp forest left and people took action. Divers, employed by kelp harvesting companies, used hammers, quicklime pellets and suction dredgers to rid the sea floor of thousands upon thousands of urchins. The campaign was considered reasonably successful, if expensive, and some of the devastated kelp forests are now recovering. In addition, since 1970 red sea urchins have been harvested for their roe which is sold as a delicacy in Japan. The market is steadily increasing and today about 1000 tonnes of sea urchins are landed annually, helping to keep urchin populations in check.

Living on the rocky seabed with the sea urchins are numerous sponges and sea anemones, and more secretive animals such as brittlestars that live in cracks and holdfasts and emerge at night to feed. Dependent on this plethora of bottom-living animals are larger creatures, such as the sheephead wrasse found along the coast of California from Monterey to Mexico. This fish is easy to identify at all stages of its life, for the juvenile, female and male are all brightly and distinctly coloured. Soon after the young fish leave the plankton, where they have lived as larvae, they become orange with a white line running horizontally along their side, and sport large black spots on their fins. Gradually over the ensuing weeks, the colours fade, the line and

LEFT: Periodically, sea urchin numbers increase dramatically and cannot be sustained by the available drift kelp.

RIGHT: The resulting devastation of the living forest is descriptively called an urchin barren.

the spots disappear and the fish look more rosy red than orange. As adults, the females are rosy red with a white chin. Males also have a white chin but the rest of the body is very dark, almost black, with a broad crimson band around the middle. In addition, the male has a large lump on his forehead, which contrasts greatly with the sloping forehead of the female.

Sheephead wrasse can grow up to nearly 1 metre (3.3 feet) long, and are the largest of all eastern Pacific wrasses. They have large, protruding teeth which give them a rather goofy appearance but are excellent for tackling the fish's hard-shelled prey. Sheephead wrasse forage on the seabed for crustaceans such as barnacles and crabs, molluscs including abalone, and sea urchins. The wrasse uses its head to bump an urchin from the rock and expose its vulnerable underside. In doing so, the fish is often pierced by a number of the urchin's spines, and it is not uncommon to see a sheephead wrasse with spines sticking out of its head. In areas where this fish is common, urchins tend to seek the shelter of cracks in the rock much of the time, limiting their grazing. But in many areas populations of sheephead wrasse have been depleted, because this fish is popular with anglers and spearfishermen, and is often used as bait in commercial traps.

There are two other predators of sea urchins that can come to the aid of the kelp forest. Typically a scavenger, the bat star will also attack small white sea urchins. This fleshy starfish uses its tube feet to overturn the urchin and expose its vulnerable underside. The starfish then turns its stomach inside out over the urchin, and digests and absorbs it, leaving only the spines and the skeleton as waste. Paradoxically, bat stars also graze rocks, preventing the successful growth of tiny new kelp plants. Using the same technique as the bat star, the larger sunflower starfish tackles the bigger, more destructive red and purple sea urchins.

One important aspect of a forest, in the sea as on land, is that it provides shelter. Within the kelp, animals are protected to a certain extent from storms and other harsh conditions, and from predators. As we found on occasion whilst diving in the forests, it is very easy to lose sight of each other in the voluminous canopy. Animals of all descriptions hide in it, both from their predators and from their prey.

Juvenile fish are generally vulnerable and tend to congregate away from open water, in mangroves, estuaries, lagoons and kelp forests. Such places are termed fish nurseries which may imply wrongly that there are adult fish looking after the young ones. In fact, they are on their own and the juvenile fish of the kelp forest and surrounding rocky reefs rely on the protection offered by the canopy. The kelp also provides plentiful and easy pickings for small fish. Many of them feed on plankton and some, such as the blacksmiths and the blue rockfish, remain in midwater as adults and continue to eat the plentiful supply of plankton that drifts by.

Whenever we looked up through the kelp forest to the surface, blacksmiths speckled the water in their search for plankton. They are very common and no less lovely for that, being more bluey grey than black, with lots of black spots along their backs.

Blacksmiths fill a similar niche in the kelp forest to the small brightly coloured fish that teem in their thousands over the coral reefs of the Caribbean, Australia and elsewhere. Blacksmiths live in dispersed schools while searching for quite large plankton, crustaceans, very small squid and even small fish. The school contracts when they are being threatened by a predator or when they are being cleaned by fish called señoritas.

The golden, cigar-shaped señoritas occur in schools that number from just a few fish to many hundreds. They forage between the seabed and the upper canopy during the day, and at night they bury themselves in the sand for safety. Señoritas play a vital role in the kelp forest. Not only do they clean fish, which queue up for the honour by hanging patiently upside down in midwater with fins splayed, they also clean the kelp plant itself. Without fish such as señoritas to keep a check on them, small barnacles, scallops and bryozoans (sea mats) would quickly cover the kelp blades. These animals use the plant's upper blades as an elevated platform from which to filter out minute particles of food from the water. If barnacles and scallops remain undetected, they will eventually weigh the blade down so much that it sinks away from the vital sunlight. Bryozoans pose even more of a threat, for they are colonial animals and spread as a white lacy growth across the blade. A heavily encrusted blade becomes so weighed down and brittle that it is very susceptible to storm damage. The blanket of bryozoans also blocks out some of the light needed by the blade for photosynthesis. Older kelp blades are often so coated they appear white, and are almost always ragged. By picking off such animals, señoritas allow the blades some respite from the inexorable process of encrustation and decay.

Larger fish also lurk in the kelp forest, and many of these rely on camouflage to get close to their prey. One of the most cleverly disguised is the giant kelpfish, an elongated and largely kelp-coloured fish that grows to about 60 centimetres (24 inches) in length. Drifting quietly in the kelp canopy, being washed to and fro with the surge, it is perfectly hidden. Not only is it shaped like a blade, its mottled colouring produces an effect much like dappled sunlight on the kelp. Furthermore, it has small white dots over its back that mimic the bryozoans found on kelp blades. Like a chameleon, it can change colour to match its background. Giant kelpfish that live in eel grass, for example, are bright green with silvery stripes, while those inhabiting red algae are an appropriate shade of maroon. Small crustaceans and fish, such as young señoritas and kelp perch, that stray too close to the giant kelpfish stand little chance of evading this invisible predator. It is, of course, equally safe from detection by its own predators.

LEFT: An opportunistic orange garibaldi waits as a male sheephead wrasse breaks up an urchin.
RIGHT: Giant kelp fish are ambush predators, relying on camouflage.

The kelp crab is similarly coloured to match the kelp, but its camouflage is for protection against its predators, rockfish and sea otters, rather than to ambush prey. It lives in the canopy, where it is difficult to see, and is also found on the stipes and around the holdfasts. It feeds on the kelp plant itself during spring when the blades are young and tender. Later on in the year, when the blades have their white blanket of bryozoans, the crabs pick away at this easily obtainable food.

A crab's hard outer covering or exoskeleton does not stretch and so it has to moult to increase in size. The new exoskeleton is soft at first and, until it hardens, the crab is vulnerable to all sorts of predators. Strangely, during the first day of its moult the kelp crab's camouflage is undeveloped and the crab is a brilliant red, making it extremely visible. Red is a colour commonly used by poisonous animals to warn off would-be predators. So the crab's hue may serve as a toxic warning signal, in this case a false one.

The equally vivid garibaldi or ocean goldfish retains its bright colouring all year, even when breeding. This fish seems to go out of its way to advertise its presence, being an almost luminous orange colour. Against the backdrop of delicate shades of greens, blues and ambers, it is impossible to ignore. The sexes look identical and both hold territories in the kelp, although the males are more tenacious than the females. Each territory includes a feeding area, a shelter hole for sleeping in and, in the case of the males, a breeding site. In the breeding season between May and October, the males stay closer to the rocky seabed and each establishes a nesting area which he will fiercely defend. He clears everything away from this patch of rock except for one particular kind of red alga. This he farms and even collects more of it from surrounding rocks. Once the nest is ready, the male tries to entice a female down to lay her eggs. When a female swims by, he ducks three times to signal to her. If she is impressed by his ducking, she swims down, lays her yellow eggs in the nest of red algae and leaves. He fertilises her eggs by swimming over them releasing sperm. He then cleans the nest, tends the eggs and protects them against predators until they hatch. Duties done, he returns to foraging more widely within his territory, browsing on sponges, bryozoans, sea slugs and small crabs under the shielding canopy.

The world's smallest marine mammals use the kelp canopy for shelter in a completely different way. Sea otters, among the most endearing creatures of the Californian kelp forests, wrap themselves up in the surface canopy at night. There, secure in their tangled and enveloping blankets, they can remain anchored for the night hidden from their predators. Kelp is so important to them that during the winter, when the kelp decays, they will compete for the remaining patches.

One evening we took a small boat to the kelp to witness the otters' night-time preparations. We were particularly fascinated by a female otter that had a small pup on her stomach. This bundle of alternately soggy and dry fluffy fur cannot have been more than 30 centimetres (12 inches) long. The mother cleaned both herself and her pup meticulously. She then sat vertically in the water with her paws held up. She picked up a tangle of kelp with her tail and legs, lay back in the water and rolled around and around until she was well anchored. The pup lay asleep with its head on her chest, completely oblivious of us throughout this operation. The mother allowed us to approach to within a couple of metres and then slowly swam away, dragging her pup with her through the kelp.

No one is sure whether sea otters give birth to their pups on land or in the water, but it is thought that they stay at sea within the protecting kelp, if possible. At birth a pup already has a covering of thick fur, essential for its survival, but it is otherwise virtually helpless and depends entirely on its mother. When the mother dives for food, the pup simply floats on the surface, hidden in the kelp and buoyed up by the air trapped in its coat. This dependency lasts for months, possibly up to a year in places where food is scarce. The father plays no role in caring for its offspring, having only spent a short period, up to three days, with the mother when they mated. Indeed, the sexes only come together to mate, living separately for most of the year.

Otters are social animals, and congregate in the kelp during the daytime to rest as well as at night to sleep. They paddle with their hind flippers when floating on their backs at the surface, using their long tapering tail as a rudder. They feed alone, dispersing through the kelp forest to seek their prey. Underwater they are supremely agile and move by undulating the lower part of their bodies up and down rather like dolphins, although otters can only achieve a top speed of 8 km/h (5 mph).

Unlike other marine mammals, sea otters have no layer of subcutaneous fat or blubber to keep them warm. They stay in the water virtually 24 hours a day, year in year out, and their fur is their only means of maintaining body heat. So their coat is much denser than that of other marine mammals, being twice the density of, for example, the Alaska fur seal's. They groom their wonderfully soft and very thick fur constantly to maintain its insulating properties.

Their lack of blubber also means that otters have no food store and as a result they have a rapacious appetite. They have to eat a quarter of their own body weight each day and spend a great deal of their time diving for food. Sea otters eat crabs, sea urchins and fish, although dealing with a slippery fish can be hard work and only the larger, stronger adults eat them regularly. Sea otters also eat abalone and have

LEFT: Sea otters gather together in the evening and wrap themselves in kelp which anchors them for the night.
RIGHT: Brilliant orange in the kelp, a solitary garibaldi patrols its territory.

marvellous ways of handling this obstinate food source. They have an extra bone in their wrist which they use, much as a diver uses an ab bar, to prise the abalone off the rock. The other way otters collect abalone is by using a small rock, for they are among the few animals, other than humans, that have mastered the art of using tools. They pick up a rock off the seabed and bash it repeatedly against the abalone until it slowly releases its hold. Several dives might be necessary to free the abalone completely, but if the otter does succeed its reward is a fat, juicy meal.

Otters will also use a rock as an anvil to crack open their hard-shelled prey. At the surface, they place the rock on their flat chest and, with both front paws, pound the shell, crab or urchin against the anvil until they can yank the flesh out with their teeth. It is an extraordinarily efficient way of extracting meat and a clever adaptation, but it does take its toll in the long run. The continual pounding against the sea otter's chest injures its sternum and ribs, which protect its heart. Older sea otters often have badly damaged chests and as a result are thought to die of heart failure.

We obtained our best views of sea otters at Monterey, where they feed in the harbour and along the shore. In addition, the aquarium in Monterey tends orphaned otters in a carefully constructed tide pool adjacent to the building before reintroducing them to the wild. In the early days, the orphans maintain close contact with their surrogate mother, a researcher. Their natural food is placed in the tide pool so that the orphans can discover and learn how to deal with it. The tide pool has open access to the sea allowing the young otters to come and go as they please, and they are encouraged to do just that. Wild otters can also enter and some do, the huge temptation of food overcoming their fear of people. One particular adult female made frequent use of this free food supply, and her visits were not discouraged because they brought the orphans into contact with a wild animal. It was this otter that we befriended.

It took us a while to work out how to keep her attention. Too much teasing frustrated her and we lost her to the kelp for a while. Gradually we learned how to play with her and became very successful at maintaining her interest. She became so accustomed to us that she would continue playing quite happily even when the camera accidentally bumped her. If she headed off, all I had to do was slap the water with my hand to attract her attention and bring her back. Within seconds she would be climbing all over me, exploring me with her soft paws and inquisitive whiskers.

The dexterity of sea otters never ceased to amaze us. They find food as they scrabble around in the often murky water by touch rather than by sight, and can differentiate between rocks, clams, abalone and other objects. They then pick up their prey and tuck it under their left foreleg, the right foreleg being the one preferred for more intricate tasks. They generally dive for a minute or two, foraging from the shallows down to 55 metres (180 feet), but they can manage several minutes underwater in an emergency to escape predators such as sharks.

As well as ably manipulating a rock, otters will use one shell against another as a tool. We observed this when we attracted the wild otter away from the aquarium's tide pool. After a dive she came up with two clams. She placed one on her chest and, using it as an anvil, cracked open and ate the other. She dived again and we thought she had forgotten, and therefore lost, the one on her chest. In fact, she had tucked the clam under her foreleg and dived for a rock on which to break it open.

Not everyone has found sea otters so delightful and fascinating. Their thick fur was coveted by people, and otters were hunted to near extinction from the mid-1700s to the early 1900s. California's population was reduced to under 100, and only by government protection and the establishment of a sea otter refuge in 1938 has it survived at all. The population is now well over 1000 and still increasing. Although sea otters do not migrate, they do tend to wander long distances and their distribution is slowly expanding every year.

There are those who resent the comeback of the sea otter, particularly the abalone fishermen. They believe that sea otters eat about 2 million US dollars' worth of shellfish off the Californian coast every year, but official estimates are vastly lower. The battle between the conservationists and the fishermen continues to rage. As a compromise, 'No Otter Zone' areas have been designated, but catching and relocating otters out of these zones is no easy task. As the population expands and spreads, the difficulty will increase.

The sea otters' voracious appetite means that they do have a major impact on their preferred food items, but in some cases this is welcomed. The urchin infestations of the kelp forests earlier this century are thought to have been at least partly due to the decimation of otters by the fur hunters. The otters' preference for the easily collected urchin now helps to keep urchin populations under control and to preserve the kelp forests. In Alaska the relationship is clear; wherever sea otters abound, sea urchins are less common and kelp forests are extensive. In California the situation is compounded by other factors, such as very destructive winter storms on its exposed coasts and higher levels of pollution. Even so, sea otters undeniably contribute to the well-being of the kelp forests there.

OVERLEAF: A moulting harbour seal avoids the rising tide until the last possible moment.

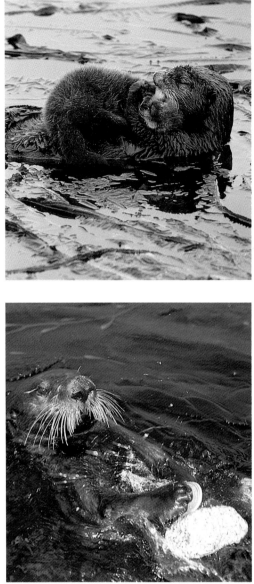

ABOVE: Buoyed up by air trapped in her fine coat, a sea otter cradles her sleeping pup.
BELOW: A sea otter cracks open its hard-shelled prey, in this case a clam, using a rock from the seabed as an anvil.

Other furred mammals found in the kelp forest include sea lions and seals. We had some encounters with sea lions in California but none to match our experiences in the Galápagos Islands. Harbour (or common) seals were much more in evidence around the kelp forest. They, and indeed all seals, differ from sea lions in having no ears, using their hind flippers rather than their foreflippers for propulsion, and in the coat. Seals have two layers of hair: a fine, soft undercoat and on top of that coarse, longer guard hairs to protect the fur. The hair of harbour seals changes colour throughout the year. When they moult, they get a new coat that is mottled black, white and silver. As the year progresses it turns brown, providing a better camouflage against predators.

Unlike sea otters, harbour seals have a great deal of blubber to help keep them warm. Half of their body weight is blubber, so that even in near-freezing water their core temperature remains constant. This allows them to inhabit arctic waters as well as California's temperate waters, and as a result they are one of the most widely distributed seals.

Other adaptations have contributed to their success. In order to maintain the blubber layer, harbour seals have to eat a lot. They are formidable hunters and eat octopus, squid, crustaceans and, primarily, a great variety of fish. Those living in or near a kelp forest have a plentiful supply of fish in relatively shallow waters. In other areas, harbour seals may have to dive down to 300 metres (1000 feet) or more in search of prey. Their eyes are adapted to gather the maximum amount of light so that they can see in the near-darkness encountered at such depths. Although their lungs are not particularly big, they can stay underwater for up to 25 minutes. This is because their blood is rich in haemoglobin and can carry two to three times as much oxygen as that of an equivalent sized land mammal. Also, during a dive the seals slow their heart rate and change the distribution of their blood, so that it flows and delivers oxygen only to the essential organs, the brain and heart, rather than to other organs and muscles.

Among the animals that prey on harbour seals are great white sharks and killer whales. The threat of such hunters makes these seals very social, for group vigilance is more effective than individual watchfulness. By remaining in groups, both when resting in the water and when sprawled on rocks, each seal is more likely to be made aware of and evade an attacker.

There is no hierarchy within the group, but there is a great deal of snorting and growling, head butting and flipper waving, as each seal establishes its own place on the rocks. When the tide comes in and begins to cover their comfortable rock, harbour seals seem to enter the water reluctantly. They may then go in search of food or merely bob around in the water. At such times, the young harbour seals play, for this is how they acquire their hunting skills and develop their stamina. Groups of playmates are usually matched in age and size which tends to reduce the risk of injury. During their first few months the pups are small and vulnerable, and restrict their play to rolling and sliding in the mud. As they become more robust, their antics become more boisterous. From one to four years of age, they play in a number of ways, including slapping the surface of the water with their tails and flippers, leaping out of the water, and simply rolling around in the water, nipping and snapping at each other like puppies.

While the sharks that attack harbour seals tend to remain offshore, some of their smaller relatives inhabit the floor of the kelp forest and the sand flats in between. One of these species, which looks more like a ray than a shark, is the angel shark. This is a very distinctive shark which has a large flattened body which grows up to 1.5 metres (5 feet) long, has very wide pectoral fins (which are not joined to the head as in rays), and has its mouth at the very front of its head. It is highly likely that we swam above angel sharks on more than one occasion without even seeing them for they are extremely well camouflaged. They lie buried in the sand much of the time and their back is a mottled pale brown. When we did find one, in water only 10 metres (33 feet) deep, we approached it very slowly in order not to disturb it. After having a good look at the shark, we got a little too close whereupon it rose out of the sand and swam off. To our surprise, its escape aroused other angel sharks hidden nearby, and soon a squadron of sharks was gliding away over the sand. Angel sharks often congregate, although they usually do so at greater depths than the ones we found. There are many reported sightings of them lying littered around a small area, virtually lying on top of one another.

We had nothing to fear from the angel sharks for they are shy creatures. They are, however, very effective predators. Their ability to lie motionless in the sand for hours and hours enables them to ambush unsuspecting prey. Angel sharks attack fish that swim too close with lightning speed, striking upwards and impaling the prey on their many small teeth. When the quiet of the sea floor is disturbed by an eruption of sand, it is often an angel shark grabbing a meal. They also feed on crustaceans and molluscs, and even other sharks

An even smaller shark we encountered, particularly at night, was the horn shark, which usually grows up to 80 centimetres (31 inches) long. Docile animals, they hide amongst the rocks during the day, well camouflaged by their mottled coloration.

LEFT: An angelshark lies hidden in the sand awaiting unsuspecting prey. As the squid passes over, the shark lunges, thrusting its jaws forward to engulf its victim.

RIGHT, ABOVE: The leopard shark is one of the few sharks to bear such prominent markings. RIGHT, BELOW: Small and vulnerable, the juvenile horn shark relies on camouflage for protection.

Horn sharks emerge at night to feed on crustaceans, sea urchins and sometimes small fish. They do not swim very well, but can move across sandy bottoms by undulating their body and can even clamber across the rocks using their strong pectoral fins almost as legs.

Their name comes from two spines at the front of both dorsal fins. In some individuals the spines take on the colour of the shark's main prey. For example, if the prey is purple sea urchins, as is often the case, the spines are purple. All the other hard parts of the shark, including its teeth, will also become stained with purple. The function of the spines is to protect the horn shark against larger predators, such as angel sharks. After a successful attack on a horn shark, it is not long before the spines are felt and the victim is spat out unharmed. The sad twist is that the spines encourage rather than deter attack by humans. The spines are sought for use in jewellery, and obviously the shark is killed in the process.

We came across a few of the horn shark's peculiar egg cases, each of which looks rather like a corkscrew. It is conical, about 15 centimetres (6 inches) long, and has two spiral lips, or flanges, that wind down around the outside. The female shark lays an egg in a soft, light brown case, picks it up in her mouth and puts it in a crack in the rock. The flanges prevent the egg case from being pulled out. In seawater, the egg case slowly darkens and hardens, further securing it in the rock. The female lays a number of eggs at the same time and may jam them all in the same crack. The wide end of the cone is not sealed, and so allows fresh oxygenated seawater to flow freely through to the developing shark. It also allowed us to open the end of a case and see the tiny shark still attached to its nutritious yolk sac without harming it in any way. After eight or nine months, the young shark has used up all the food in the yolk sac, and is on the point of hatching. When it wriggles out of its case, it is about 20 centimetres (8 inches) long and extremely vulnerable.

Almost anything will eat such a small delicate creature, including leopard sharks. These are sleek, silky looking sharks, covered in large, very regular dark bars and spots. On Catalina, one of the more populated Channel Islands, there is a cove where leopard sharks sometimes gather in their dozens. When we walked along this shore, we were amazed to be able to count well over 50 sharks, their dorsal fins breaking the surface. No one is quite sure why they do this and a research programme has been started in Catalina to look into it. Leopard sharks do congregate in shallow water to reproduce, but we were there in August, long after the normal breeding season. It may be that some populations have a split breeding season. Another theory is that the sharks are attracted by the water temperature. Sharks are cold-blooded, and therefore their metabolism is to some extent governed by the temperature of the water. In a shallow, protected cove where there are no currents, the water is a few degrees warmer than in the open ocean. In warmer water their metabolism may increase just a little, and this might allow pregnant females to reduce the time they have to carry their litters. Without thorough investigation this idea merely remains one of conjecture.

Another bottom-dwelling creature of the kelp forest that we were keen to meet up with was the bat ray. Rays are related to sharks, but look very different from most sharks having wide, flat bodies with wing-like pectoral fins. While most rays have a flat head with eyes on the top, the dramatic-looking bat ray has a thick, raised head with eyes on the side. In the event, we rarely got close to a bat ray and when we did it was usually to our surprise. We found them skittish, the slightest movement making them glide away.

Bat rays specialise in eating hard-shelled prey, such as mussels, oysters, clams and crabs. Like other rays and sharks, bat rays can locate prey hidden from sight by detecting the electric fields they generate. Bat rays also rise to the abalone challenge. Using their very strong, crushing jaws they simply bite the abalone off the rock. This action is in stark contrast to the almost ethereal image they present as they fly through the kelp forest. Of all the animals we saw in the kelp, the bat rays were by far the most graceful. We would glimpse them taking off from a sand patch, and then watch as they flew through the forest with a fluency and ease that was arresting.

One of the most magnificent spectacles in the kelp forest occurs early in the summer when bat rays come together in huge numbers to mate. Hundreds of rays whirl in great schools looking for a partner. From time to time during the courtship swim, a male will chase a female away from the group and try to mate with her. She may acquiesce or she may refuse and swim back to join the school once again.

Kelp forests are not isolated from the open ocean and many animals move between the two habitats. Some do so daily such as the sea lions which hunt primarily outside the kelp forests, and may snatch a quick bite within them on their way. Much smaller animals of the kelp forest may take an involuntary and possibly one-way trip to the ocean with kelp rafts, such as those we saw on our journeys between the various Channel Islands. Storms often set kelp plants adrift, leaving them to float away from the shallows into the ocean where they remain at the mercy of the currents. Kelp rafts can be small straggling mats of fronds and blades, or they can extend for tens of metres. Both underneath and on the unfortunate kelp plant reside many animals typical of the kelp forest. Those animals that are attached to the plant have little

choice about whether they stay or go. More mobile animals that are closely associated with kelp plants in the forest, such as little crabs and young fish, may remain under the protective canopy as it drifts away and find themselves in the unfamiliar territory of the deep ocean.

Much of the life on the rafts falls prey to pelagic (open ocean) predators en route, but some may survive until the raft is washed shoreward again. If the new location provides suitable conditions, these survivors may be able to colonise it. Just as vegetation rafts from the American mainland carried animals to the Galápagos Islands, so kelp rafts assist in the colonisation of islands. They are also a means by which populations of the same species, living separately around the margins of the ocean, can intermix.

Drifting kelp is also used as a shelter by animals of the open ocean. Juvenile pelagic fish will temporarily seek the refuge offered by the raft and they, in turn, attract larger fish which prey on them. In this way the kelp raft builds up its own transitory community. Visiting birds arrive from time to time to rest on the rafts and probably to feed from them too, and sea gulls often act as good markers of rafts out at sea.

Sunfish are one of the stranger open ocean species that may be found under kelp rafts. We first came across them in their more usual surroundings, basking at the surface. I had never seen sunfish before, and found them an astonishing sight. They seem to lack the posterior section of their body altogether. The short tail, more like a flap, and the very long dorsal and anal fins, both of which are set far back along the body, give the fish its misshapen appearance. Their deep bodies look almost circular from side on and very thin from front or back. Like many pelagic fish, sunfish have a darker bluey grey back and a whiter underside. They have no snout to speak of, and a small mouth with no teeth. Instead of scales they are encased in skin that has a thick mucous covering and contains an unpleasant tasting chemical called tetrodotoxin. Also found in other fish, this toxin is an effective defence against predators. The bizarre-looking sunfish can reach an impressive 4 metres (13 feet) in length and can weigh as much as 1 tonne. This bulk is built up on a diet of jellyfish and other watery gelatinous animals.

Sunfish live in the surface waters of the oceans but will dive deep when alarmed, as we soon found out. Time and time again we tried to approach them in the water, and only once or twice did we get close before they descended out of our range. By chance one may see them in the kelp forest occasionally, for during the late summer

In early summer, bat rays gather in vast numbers to mate.

The bizarre looking ocean sunfish is usually encountered basking near the surface.

some are washed in by ocean currents. Looking very out of place in the kelp, they take the opportunity of being cleaned by señoritas before making their way back to the ocean.

We encountered the sunfish while seeking a much more fearsome animal. Blue sharks spend nearly all their time in open waters but sometimes patrol the edge of the kelp forest for an easy meal. We did not see them there, though, and so we had journeyed out to their blue water home in search of them. Blue sharks can reach 3.4 metres (11 feet) in length and for safety we had to mount a serious 'shark operation', involving a cage, shark suits, bait and bang sticks.

The long pectoral fins and streamlining of the blue shark make it an extremely graceful long-distance swimmer.

Shark suits are made of chain mail and are heavy, difficult to get on, difficult to work in – and necessary. When wearing them on board, we had to move round with great caution for they are very slippery. If one of us had slipped off the boat, the suit would have acted as an irremovable weight of over 8 kilograms (18 pounds) that would have taken the diver straight down to the bottom of the ocean. The chain mail has zero stretchability and hindered movement, swimming and comfort to a greater extent than we had expected. Even reaching down to get flippers on was a struggle. In the water, the suits greatly increased our surface area, creating massive drag and making diving an exhausting activity.

The bait for the sharks was frozen fish hung over the side of the boat in a crate. It took a while for the sharks to pick up the scent and sometimes we had to wait an hour or two before the first one arrived. But without fail, after a few hours we attracted between five and ten sharks. The cage was then lowered into the water and allowed to drift away from the boat to the end of its line. It was there for us to escape into but we never needed a refuge and used it instead as a reference point underwater.

As an additional precaution, some safety divers had bang sticks to keep the sharks off the cameraman. A loaded bang stick acts like a gun and will kill a shark dead if fired. Fortunately, the ones we used never had to be loaded, a gentle tap being all that was required to deter the sharks.

All thoughts of discomfort disappeared when the subjects of the operation appeared on the scene. Blue sharks, named for the iridescent blue along their backs, are sleek, streamlined, elegant creatures. They have exceptionally long pectoral fins which are ideal for sustained cruising. These sharks are curious, sometimes frisky and we were repeatedly bumped, nosed, mouthed and bitten. As they continued to bite, we became increasingly grateful for the protection of our shark suits. Sometimes, alarmingly, their teeth would get caught in the chain mail, but a quick thrash of their tail set them free again. We were usually surrounded by sharks no more than 2 metres (6.6 feet) long, but one or two seemed, and indeed were, huge.

Blue sharks are one of the most abundant large animals on Earth. They are probably the most common of all the open water sharks, being found in temperate and subtropical seas worldwide. They are also one of the most itinerant sharks, tagged individuals having crossed the Atlantic. Blue sharks are thought to use oceanic currents to travel such long distances. They prefer cooler seas, where they tend to stay in shallow water, and may venture closer to land at night to feed. In tropical water, they can usually be found at depths of 60 metres (200 feet) or more, where the water temperature is low.

In order to remain in midwater without continually swimming to maintain position, an animal needs to be close to neutral buoyancy. Sharks have a skeleton made of cartilage rather than the heavier bone. In addition, the blue shark has a particularly large oily liver that can make up 20 per cent of its body weight. This oil is much less dense than water. As a result, the weight of a blue shark in water is substantially reduced from what it would otherwise be.

The sharks planed so smoothly through the water that they seemed to move with unhurried grace. This was a false impression for blue sharks can maintain a cruising speed of 40 km/h (25 mph) and attain 70 km/h (44 mph) in short chases. Like other sharks, they use the tail for thrust and the pectoral fins for turning. They feed primarily on small fish such as sardines, anchovies, herring, mackerel, haddock and flyingfish, and, at night near the surface, on squid. Their mouths are small, and their serrated, backward-pointing teeth are ideal for dealing with such prey. Smaller animals, such as shrimp, that might otherwise escape, are trappd by the sharks' finely meshed gills.

The sharks' black eyes were most unnerving and seemed almost flawless in their clarity. Good vision is even more vital for fast-swimming hunters than for bottom-dwelling predators, such as the angel shark. To increase the sensitivity of their eyes in the dimly lit water, blue sharks use a similar system to that of nocturnal mammals such as cats. A layer of mirror-like cells at the back of the eye, called the tapetum, reflects 90 per cent of the light back to the light receptor cells. So the eyes get a second chance to register the light, and form a clearer image of the scene. Many sharks, including the blue shark, have an extra fold of skin on the lower lid called a nictitating membrane. Unlike the lid itself, the membrane is movable and closes over the eye as the shark comes to bite, protecting the eye from any damage that might be inflicted by a thrashing victim.

All the sharks we swam with were males, apart from one female, for in summer most females move north to colder water. This solitary female was badly scarred. Scarring is found on many female sharks and is the result of biting by males during courtship and mating. The bites can be quite severe, and the female blue shark has skin two to three times thicker than the male's – and thicker than the male's teeth are long – for protection. The embryo sharks, each surrounded by an egg membrane, grow in separate compartments in the uterus. After 9 to 12 months, the mother gives birth to up to 100 live young in open water. Once born, like horn sharks, the young are on their own. They often separate into groups according to size and sex, which seems to be a way of reducing predation by both older sharks and male sharks on the young.

While blue sharks stay mainly in the open ocean, the kelp forests are important to them. As well as providing the occasional easy meal for those that stray inshore, the forests act as a refuge for the young of many of the fish on which the sharks depend. By providing so much living space and protection, the kelp forests help to maintain a high fish productivity along the Californian coast to the benefit of man as well as sharks and other marine animals. They also allow a much greater diversity of life to inhabit the coast than would otherwise be possible. In their turn, the innumerable animals that grace these waters, from jewel-like anemones to sea otters, sharks and whales, enhance the inherent beauty of the forest's maze of vivid amber vines.

AUSTRALIA'S
GREAT BARRIER REEF

Rocks and shoals are always dangerous to the mariner, even where their situation has been ascertained; they are more dangerous in seas which have never before been navigated, and in this part of the globe they are more dangerous than in any other.
Captain James Cook, 1770.

I felt rather differently on viewing the Great Barrier Reef, but then I am a diver, not a mariner. I found the reef overwhelming in its size, and in the variety of its life, form and colour.

The only way to appreciate the vastness of the Great Barrier Reef is to view it from an aeroplane or, better still, from space. For the Great Barrier Reef is not one reef, but a chain of reefs that extends some 2300 kilometres (1400 miles) from the Gulf of Papua in the north to the Tropic of Capricorn in the south, and covers an area larger than Great Britain. The barrier is made up of over 2500 individual reefs of all sizes, varying from as large as 130 square kilometres (50 square miles) to mere isolated pinnacles. In addition, within the barrier are 540 continental islands, most of them fringed by reefs.

A view from the sky also reveals the intricate patchwork

A coral cay with its reef clearly visible against the deeper water.

of colours that make up the barrier, ranging from blues, turquoises and aquamarines to a variety of greens. These changes in colour are largely due to changes in the depth of the water. Out on the edge of the ocean, the water is a clean dark blue, while in shallower sea the sand beneath reflects light making the water appear turquoise. In-shore water receives more vegetation from the land and so looks greener. The reefs appear rather like rocks surrounded by shallow water, the white of breaking waves marking their seaward edge. Within the shallow lagoons of some reefs, sand has built up into a small island or cay which may have vegetation shading its centre.

Perhaps the single most incredible facet of the barrier is that this enormous structure has been constructed by the combined efforts of corals and single-celled algae. Corals often look like plants, growing in the shape of plates, crusts, domes and shrubs, yet they feel like rocks, and are, in fact, animals. They belong to a group called the coelenterates, which also includes jellyfish and anemones. All these animals have certain features in common, such as only having one opening which serves as both a mouth and an anus, and stinging cells for catching prey. The term 'corals' is often used to refer to just the hard or stony corals, which may build up to form reefs. There are many other types that share the same basic form such as soft corals, stinging or fire corals, black corals and sea fans or gorgonians.

The hard, reef-building corals consist of colonies of tiny animals known as polyps. A coral polyp is basically a fleshy cylinder with an open top ringed by tentacles. Food enters through the top and waste passes out the same way. There are three layers in the walls of the 'cylinder': the inner layer has glands and digests the food, the middle is the 'jelly' of the animal, and the outer layer builds up calcium carbonate crystals to form the coral skeleton. The needle-shaped crystals are bundled together into fans, and these are stacked up in rods which form the framework of the coral. Each coral polyp lives within, and is supported by, its own calcium carbonate cup. In the same way that a tree's growth rings show the conditions experienced by that tree, so the crystals in a coral are banded and can be used as a calendar of events in the sea.

Most people are familiar with the pure white skeletons of dead corals left after the polyps have been cleaned out. Underwater, the living corals come in a variety of colours including pink, green, blue, purple and beige. It is the live part of the coral that is coloured, forming just a thin layer on the surface of the skeleton below. The colours are partly due to the millions of single-celled algae living within each polyp. Like all plants, these microscopic algae photosynthesise, producing oxygen and food from carbon dioxide and water. Both the coral and the algae benefit from living together. The coral gains oxygen and a great deal of food. Most importantly, without

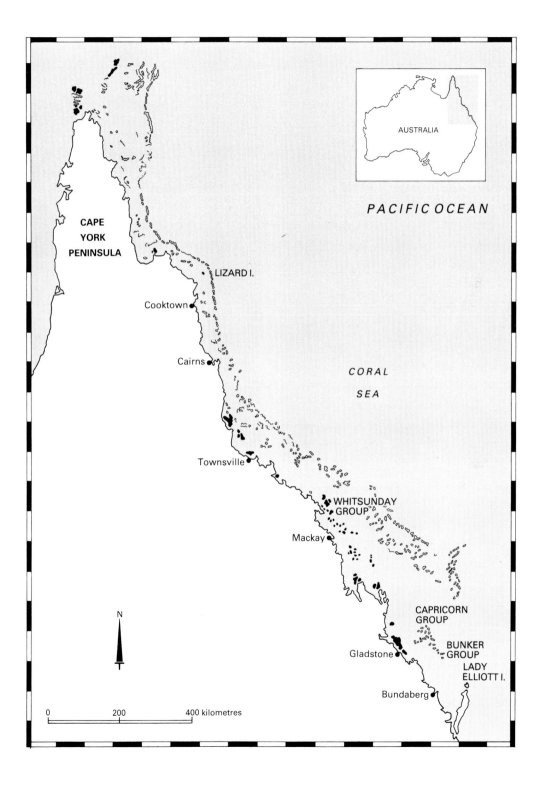

ABOVE, LEFT: Whip-like corals flourish in deeper water.
ABOVE, RIGHT: A rich diversity of coral forms.

OPPOSITE, ABOVE: Gorgonian polyps strain the water for food.
OPPOSITE, BELOW: Staghorn coral adds colour to the shallow reef.

the algae corals could not build such impressive skeletons, for the algae enhance the formation of calcium carbonate crystals. The algae gain a home and the coral's waste products from which to manufacture food. Particularly precious are the elements nitrogen and phosphorus, which are well-known constituents of fertilisers used on land plants. The warm water in which corals grow usually contains only small amounts of these elements. The recycling of nitrogen and phosphorus between the coral and the algae is efficient, with little lost to the sea.

Shallow-dwelling corals may gain almost all the food they require from the algae, but deeper corals receive too little light for their algae to manufacture much food.

So they have to rely more on catching prey from the water brought by currents. Most corals feed at night when there are fewer fish to nibble at their extended tentacles. This is also the time when the microscopic animals or zooplankton on which they feed are more abundant in the water. Corals catch prey using the stinging cells on their tentacles. Each stinging cell is a capsule holding a tightly coiled, barbed and poisonous 'harpoon'. Any stimulus, mechanical or chemical, can trigger the release of a harpoon that paralyses the prey. Then the tentacle bends inwards to transfer the food down to the mouth. Corals may also ensnare bacteria and zooplankton in mucous nets which cover the colony.

Food captured by one polyp is food for the entire colony, because the polyps are connected by tissue. Not only do they pass food from one polyp to the next, they also communicate with each other. If you touch an extended polyp it will withdraw into its cup immediately and, as the message is passed along, the rest of the colony will gradually retract. This defence prevents fish and other coral-eating animals from having access to all the polyps in a colony once they start feeding on it. It also reduces the extent of injury. Polyps are very easily damaged, and by brushing against a coral, let alone kicking it, a diver is likely to kill a number of polyps.

Some hard corals do not form colonies, but remain as single polyps throughout their lives. The largest of these is the mushroom coral, which grows to 15 centimetres (6 inches) or more. The walls supporting this giant polyp are numerous and large, and resemble the underside of a mushroom. Its tentacles are also large and look rather like worms when they are extended at night. It is surprisingly mobile for a coral and can right itself if washed upside down in a storm and may even move along the seabed.

Reef-building corals are colonial and need algae to grow well. Since algae need sunlight to photosynthesise, reefs are restricted to sunlit, shallow waters. Corals are rarely found as deep as 100 metres (330 feet) because by then over 99 per cent of the sunlight has been filtered out by the water. A coral's algae also determine its shape to a certain extent. For example, in very shallow water that receives a great deal of sun, a coral can be folded or branched, with some polyps partially shaded. In deeper water, the same species of coral may grow flat so that all its algae are able to make the most of any available light.

Reef-building corals are restricted by other factors besides the amount of sunlight they receive. To grow well, they need a water temperature between 23 and 29°C (73 and 84°F). They also prefer a certain salinity, a lack of silt, and water movement to bring nutrients and food. As a result, coral reefs are only found in certain locations around the world, occurring mainly within the tropics along the edges of continents and islands, and around the peaks of submerged mountains.

In a suitable area, colony upon colony of corals may build up into a reef over time, the living corals growing on the dead ones. The reefs that develop near the shore of continents and islands are known as fringing reefs. Where a shallow seabed extends for some way out from land, reefs may develop far out to sea. When many such reefs develop in a line parallel to, but some distance from, the shore, they form a barrier reef. Barrier reefs are not necessarily continuous, as the name might imply. The Great Barrier Reef, for example, is made up of countless smaller reefs strung out along the edge of the Australian continental shelf.

The Great Barrier's outer reefs lie between 32 and 260 kilometres (20 and 160 miles) from the mainland. The drop on their seaward edge is steep, plunging to depths of over 1000 metres (3300 feet) within just a few hundred metres of the reef edge. Because of their near vertical walls and juxtaposition to the open ocean with its crystal clear water, these reefs are wonderful to dive on. Coral growth on the crest is prolific but stunted by continuous battering from the ocean waves. Lower down, beneath the influence of normal wave action, the corals are splendid and the fish plentiful. Even the lower ramparts of a reef may be devastated by wave action, though, when a cyclone passes over.

Protected by the outer reefs lie inner reefs with sand-choked lagoons. The water is less clear inside the barrier but this has little apparent effect on coral growth. Swimming on an inner reef was like moving through a beautifully designed Japanese garden. Table corals rose up out of the reefs forming avenues, brain corals sat heavily on the rock, while delicate branching corals reached up into the water, and the younger colonies nestled in the shadow of their larger neighbours.

Geologically speaking the Great Barrier Reef is young. In the distant past, the Australian continent lay further south, near Antarctica. Gradually it drifted away from Antarctica, moving northward. For a long time, the north-east coast was in water too cold for corals to survive. Eventually it began to enter an area rich in corals, and about 18 million years ago the foundations of the present-day reef were being built. Growth has not been continuous because periods of glaciation during the Ice Ages have caused changes in sea level, exposing and killing existing reefs. Most of the Barrier Reef we see today is thought to be less than 10 000 years old.

During this relatively short space of time, countless corals have established themselves, reproduced and died, their skeletons forming the building blocks of this huge network of reefs. Yet adult corals live firmly attached to the reef, unable to move

around to find a mate or colonise a new area. So how have the corals reproduced so prolifically and spread along thousands of kilometres of coast?

A coral polyp can reproduce by dividing and then laying down a wall of calcium carbonate between the two identical polyps or clones. Each of these grows up and out, dividing repeatedly as they go. Encrusting corals grow only at the edges of the colony, while plate corals, which also grow at the edges, lift off the reef into the water. Foliose corals expand within and around the colony, forming leaf-like sheets and undulations. When the polyps of brain corals clone they do not separate completely and only form walls along their sides. Hence they grow in continuous lines reminiscent of the meandering fissures of the human brain. Branching corals keep on dividing or splitting to form new branches and in so doing, greatly increase the surface area of the colony exposed to water. Branches, weakened and then broken off by waves, may settle on the reef or the seabed and establish new colonies.

One of the advantages of spreading by cloning and breakages is that they can continue reproducing year round. A drawback is that all the 'daughter' colonies

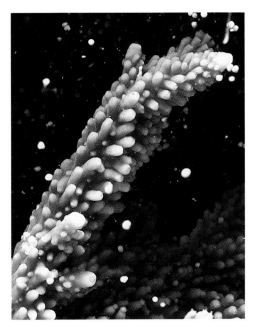

OPPOSITE: The annual synchronised spawning of corals occurs at night. The brain coral's polyp releases its package of eggs and sperm through its mouth.

ABOVE, LEFT: The buoyant bundles rise slowly to the surface. ABOVE, RIGHT: The simultaneous release of spawn by thousands of corals enhances cross-fertilisation.

formed are exactly the same as the parents. To be able to adapt to new conditions, all forms of life, including corals, need the genetic variety which comes through sexual reproduction. For this, corals produce gametes – eggs and sperm – at certain times of the year. When an egg and sperm fuse, they form a fertilised egg, which can develop into a larva and then into an adult polyp.

Some species of coral produce live young from eggs and sperm. These viviparous or live-bearing corals fertilise their own eggs internally. The larvae that hatch out are kept safe within the coral until they are well developed, and are then released into the sea. Some of these larvae can swim and may move far away from the parent colony, while others cannot and settle close by.

Until 1981, live-bearing was thought to be the main method of sexual reproduction in corals. Then it was discovered that most corals on the Great Barrier Reef reproduce by releasing a plethora of eggs and sperm into the water in the hope that some will strike lucky. This method is called broadcast spawning and is used by over 130 species of coral on the Great Barrier Reef, whereas only 46 species are viviparous. In some species of broadcast spawners, the individual coral animals are either male or female and produce only one kind of gamete, sperm or eggs. In most corals, the individual polyps are simultaneously both male and female (hermaphrodite) and release both eggs and sperm.

The most amazing aspect of coral spawning is that thousands upon thousands of corals all along the reef synchronise their reproduction so that they release their gametes at the same time. Six months before spawning, triggered by the rising water temperature in spring, the eggs start developing. Within the six weeks before their release they become coloured green, brown or, commonly, pink. The sperm are much smaller and are only visible as they become concentrated, one week before spawning. An hour or less before the release, some corals can be seen 'setting' or packaging their eggs and sperm into round bundles, one per polyp. The bundles, which appear as blobs through the transparent polyp tissues, may contain a number of eggs and/or thousands of sperm.

It is commonly said that the entire coral population of the Great Barrier Reef spawns on one or two nights a year. This is an exaggeration, for this fantastic feat of synchronisation can be split between October, November and December. The date of release of the gametes is governed by the lunar cycle, most corals spawning between the fourth and seventh night after the full moon. This is because tides become smaller after the full moon and there is less water movement across the reef, giving the gametes a better chance of finding each other before being washed away. The spawning is affected by the temperature of the water, the inshore reefs that are surrounded by shallower, warmer water spawning first, followed by those in the colder water of the outer barrier. Spawning on all reefs always occurs after dark when most of the animals that would prey on the gametes in the plankton are asleep. The exact hour of spawning is cued by darkness, and different species of coral spawn at different times between sunset and midnight. For example, all the colonies of one species may release their gametes one hour after sunset. Obviously this helps to ensure that the eggs and sperm from many different colonies of the same species meet. Also, the highly coordinated release makes the water so laden with eggs and sperm that any predators quickly become satiated and many of the gametes survive. And so, predictably, every year, in what is often called the greatest sex shown on earth, the mass synchronised spawning of corals occurs.

It was in December that we saw this event for ourselves. We stayed for some time by a large table coral which was due to spawn that night. Eventually we were rewarded by a spectacular sight, well worth the wait. As we hovered, little pink blobs started appearing in the colony, one in each coral polyp. Then, apparently all on cue, they started popping or easing out. Very quickly the water was filled with little pink balls rising slowly to the surface in such profusion that the scene resembled an inverted snowstorm. We spent over two hours in the water, fascinated, while colony after colony of different species shed their gametes.

Some colonies take up to an hour to release their gametes. Others do so in a matter of minutes by rapid contractions of the polyps. One species we saw appeared to smoke as clouds of eggs or sperm gently wafted up the water column. Almost all eggs and sperm are buoyant and float to the surface. This helps them to get away from hungry mouths, and to disperse along the reef and to other reefs. On reaching the surface the bundles soon break up and pink slicks appear on the surface of the water. Ideally each egg in the slick will fuse with a sperm from a different colony of the same species. This is known as cross-fertilisation, and the gametes are designed to increase the chances of it happening. In some species the eggs do not fully develop until they have reached the surface and started to disperse, so they are not fertilised by sperm packaged in the same bundle. The eggs and sperm contain chemical 'tags' that help them recognise others of the same species. They also seem to contain chemical inhibitors that stop the fusion of eggs and sperm from the same colony. These chemical barriers lose their effectiveness after a few hours, allowing eggs that remain unfertilised to fuse with any sperm, even those from the same colony.

Each egg starts to divide about two hours after fertilisation. Within two days the young coral has developed into a fully mobile larva which forms part of the plankton. During this larval stage of its life, the coral may be scattered over the reef and on to other reefs. How far it actually travels depends partly on how long the larva remains drifting in the plankton. Some coral larvae can survive for as long as three months in the plankton, but these are exceptions. Usually larvae settle out of the plankton on to the reef after only 4–7 days. The dispersal of larvae may also be restricted by gyres, or back eddies, around reefs which tend to keep the larvae close to the parent reef. As a result, 70 per cent of larvae settle within 300 metres (1000 feet) of their parent colonies.

Some larvae do drift away from the reef and settle in new areas. Their chances of establishing themselves fall sharply as the distance from the parent reef increases, but some do succeed. Similarly, there will be a small but steady supply of foreign larvae arriving on the parent reef. Another rather surprising way corals disperse is on floating lumps of pumice. Larvae that unwittingly settle on a piece of pumice may be transported thousands of kilometres as they grow. Only a few corals may travel in this way at any one time but over the thousands of years the Great Barrier Reef has been forming, considerable quantities of coral have been transported there from other reefs in the Pacific by floating pumice.

Once a larva has settled on the reef, it crawls to find a suitable spot and attaches itself. Then it starts the slow process of building its skeleton and cloning, each polyp in turn creating its own miniature tower. From such tiny and vulnerable beginnings as these, the entire Great Barrier Reef has grown. The complex three-dimensional structure of the reef provides a home or refuge for an enormous number of animals and plants.

The power of living and hiding places to attract a diverse community was very evident when we dived in the deep channel that runs down the inside of the reefs. It has been etched out by currents that increased in strength as the barrier grew, forcing the water into a narrower gap. Now used as a shipping lane, the channel contains the wreck of the passenger vessel *Yongala*, which sank during a cyclone in 1911 with all lives lost. Since then many marine animals have colonised the wreck. Other hurricanes and cyclones have periodically destroyed animals covering its super-structure, but these have usually been replaced within a year. Exploring the *Yongala* was as exciting as we had hoped, for a profusion of animals live there amid the unpredictable currents.

This artificial reef was completely encrusted with soft corals, hydroids, algae, sponges, bryozoans and the like. Among these attached animals swam hundreds of juvenile fish, dashing for cover as huge, silver, predatory jacks shot over the wreck. Coral trout, red with purple spots, lay in wait, ready to ambush unsuspecting prey. Eagle rays, with diamond-shaped bodies, long, thin, whip-like tails and white spots on black backs, glided effortlessly in squadrons above the bows of the wreck. They feed on shellfish and have a remarkable ability to crush their prey's hard outer casing. They then extract the flesh and spit out the unwanted fragments of shell. Slithering amongst the luxuriant growth were olive sea snakes. I picked up one of these with trepidation for this snake can deliver a venomous bite. I grasped it just behind the head, so it could not turn and bite me, and held it for only a short time because, like its land relatives, it needs to breathe air. Although it seemed very exposed as it wound its way up towards the surface of the water, its venom deters all but the larger sharks, such as tiger sharks, from preying on it.

While the wreck houses a huge variety of animals, the diversity of life on the Great Barrier Reef itself is vastly greater. It is enhanced by the wide range of habitats on offer due to the sheer distance from north to south and the varying influences of land

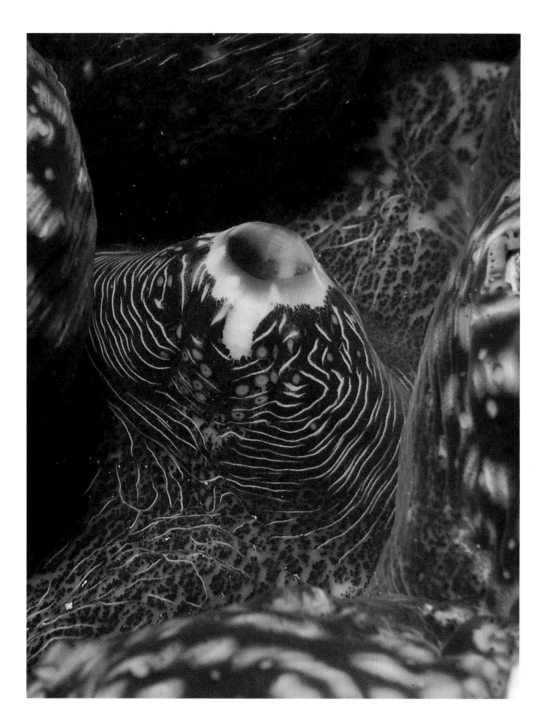

Detail of a clam's siphon.

and sea from west to east. As a result, the Great Barrier Reef boasts some 400 species of hard and soft coral, 4000 molluscs, innumerable other invertebrates and an impressive 1500 species of fish. All of these have had to develop successful ways of reproducing to ensure that their line survives in future generations.

One of the most impressive inhabitants of the reef is the giant clam, *Tridacna gigas*. This species is the largest of several giant clams found in the Pacific, and is the fastest growing bivalve in the world. It increases in length at a rate of 8–12 centimetres (3–5 inches) per year when young and can reach a grand 1.4 metres (4.6 feet) in length. As in other bivalve molluscs, such as oysters and mussels, the giant clam's body is encased in a hinged shell. Usually it lies on the seabed sieving food with shell agape, but it can partially close the shell when danger threatens. As a child, I was told horror stories about giant clams slamming their shells shut on the ankles of divers and holding them underwater until they drowned. I discovered many years later that, in fact, as these clams attain their enormous proportions, they lose their ability to shut their shells completely. Because of their size giant clams, like corals, are unable to move around in search of a mate, so they too have had to develop an alternative way of reproducing.

If such a sedentary creature was either male or female, it could find itself stuck in a sterile, single-sex community. So clams are hermaphrodites, able to act as either male or female with any neighbouring clams. But they start off life as males, only developing female parts as well when they are about six years old. This is probably because sperm, being much smaller than eggs, require far less energy to produce. The young male clam can therefore put most of its energy into growing. As it increases in size, the clam can gather more food and, hence, gain more energy, and is able to start producing energy-expensive eggs. The larger it grows, the more eggs it can produce, increasing its chances of reproducing successfully.

On the Great Barrier Reef, the giant clams spawn from early to mid-summer on those days of the lunar cycle when the tides become smaller, just as corals do. The exact day may vary between reefs, but all clams spawn in the late afternoon, cued by the fading light. As each clam spawns it releases chemicals that induce neighbouring clams to spawn. At the same time it ejects its gametes forcefully so that they rise high in the water column and spread out quickly. Both these actions increase the chances of cross-fertilisation. In addition, one clam will spawn a number of times in the breeding season, but it will not produce sperm and eggs in the same spawning. The clam usually sheds sperm first, and releases eggs, resembling grains of sand, some days or even weeks later.

We came to shallow, rather murky water to witness the impressive spectacle of a clam spawning. As we approached, our shadows passed over the clam and it retreated into its shell. Clams have eyes, sensitive to light and shade, along the edge of the mantle, which is the fleshy part of the clam that lines the edges of the shell. The mantles of clams are strikingly beautiful, crystalline pigments making them shine in iridescent spots of blues and greens. Gradually the clam opened up and the mantle became fully visible again. We could also see the hole or siphon which the clam uses to suck in food-bearing water and the smaller siphon through which the filtered water is expelled.

After a long wait, the long thin inhalant siphon contracted to a slit and the round exhalant siphon slowly closed. The animal seemed to swell up and a few little trickles of sperm oozed out and dispersed in the water. Then there was a huge blow and a thick milky white jet of sperm shot up, mushrooming above the clam. A minute or so later, it started to swell up for another burst. We were surprised by the reserves of the clam for as we watched it let off a dozen blows, each as impressive as the first.

Each fertilised egg develops into an actively swimming larva after 16 hours and after only seven days, it moves down out of the open water on to the reef. Within another three days, it has become a tiny clam. At this stage it can still move around by extending and contracting a muscular leg-like 'foot'. In this way, it locates a suitable spot to settle and spend the rest of its life.

The clam needs energy and food for growth, and spends all day pumping water to obtain oxygen and plankton. Like corals, the clam also has microscopic algae living within it which manufacture food through photosynthesis. The algae manufacture about 80 per cent of the clam's food, and so the clam's growth rate depends largely on how much sunlight its algae receive. The algae live in a layer in the mantle, and both partners benefit from this association. While the clam gets food and assistance in building its huge shell, the algae gain a home and some of the clam's waste products, which they use in making food.

Clams literally form algae, culturing them in the mantle which acts like a green-house. They also eat them, and excrete both digested and intact algae. It is from the faeces of established clams that recently hatched clams acquire their crop of algae. This may explain why clams are found in clusters, for a young clam that settles near mature ones is far more likely to acquire the vital algae than one that lodges some distance away.

For generations Pacific Islanders have gathered the reef's clams for food and for use in ceremonies. In the past, the clam's reproduction strategy maintained stocks

but now the fast-growing human population is putting more and more pressure on supplies. The problem is aggravated as clams become spread too thinly along a reef to synchronise their spawning. Nowadays the chemical cue released by a spawning clam has often become too diffuse to have any effect by the time it reaches distant neighbours. So this age-old food supply is threatened with extinction in some areas. One solution is to protect existing populations, and enhance their reproductive success by moving scattered clams together into clusters. Fortunately, clams are also excellent candidates for aquaculture. They spawn profusely in tanks, have a short larval life and require virtually no maintenance as they grow in the sunlight, first in tanks and then in seawater.

Other sought-after reef inhabitants are some of the diverse and spectacular fish found there. Unlike corals and the giant clam, fish have the luxury of being able to move around to find partners. But there is such a profusion of species scattered over the reef that it can be difficult for a fish to find another of its own kind. So a number of the reef fish are broadcast spawners too, including wrasse, basslets, groupers and butterflyfish. Apart from spawning techniques, fish have developed many other fascinating and often intricate ways of increasing reproductive success.

The cleaner wrasse is a small blue and black fish which sets up cleaning stations on the reef where other fish queue to be groomed. Like many of the smaller reef fish, it lives in harems, those of the cleaner wrasse typically consisting of up to 16 females and one dominant male. Yet all cleaner wrasse start life as females. They are territorial fish and have a hierarchy within the harem dominated by the male, who performs aggressive displays as he patrols his territory. The females have subterritories spaced within the male's, and each female is aggressive towards those more junior than herself. When the male in the harem dies or is taken by a predator, the most senior female changes sex and takes over the role of the dominant male. Within hours of his disappearance she behaves like a male, showing aggression to the other females and patrolling the territory, and within two weeks 'she' has become a 'he' and is producing sperm. The speed with which cleaner wrasse can change sex shows that the larger females are ready to be males, and are only kept as females by the continuous aggression of the male. If a male dies in an area with a high concentration of cleaner wrasse, a neighbouring male may take over instead. Then a dominant female that has started changing sex by becoming aggressive will revert to behaving

Nothing I had read or seen before prepared me for the actual size of giant clams.

like a female. A female may also change sex if the harem gets too big for the male to control. A senior female living on the periphery of the male's territory receives less aggressive attention than those near the middle. She may eventually split off with a number of junior females, establish a territory for her harem and turn into a male.

If these fish did not change sex, the males would have to wait until they themselves were fully mature before they could gain access to females and reproduce. Cleaner fish can all reproduce as females while they grow and those best adapted to survive will become the senior females and, in time, will dominate the harems as males, each having sole access to his group of reproducing females. These and other advantages have made changing sex a common strategy among reef fish. Indeed, more than 100 species of marine fish, belonging to 15 families, change from female to male or vice versa. When a female changes to a male, it often also replaces a dull colour with a brighter hue.

One of the prettiest fish that swarms over the reef is a fairy basslet, *Anthias pleurotaenia*. Its harems contain little orange fish with, amongst the schools, a few beautifully coloured purple fish of the same size. The numerous orange fish are female and the purple ones male. In some species of fairy basslets, if one of the males guarding the harem is lost, the ratio of males to females is kept constant by the dominant female turning into a male and assuming the brilliant coloration.

The moon wrasse has developed a slightly different strategy, and one that seems to depend on the size of the reef. Moon wrasse are born as either females, or males called primary males. Both are drab green in colour and are relatively unaggressive. Senior females may later change into males, known as secondary males. They then adopt a more vivid coloration, with bright pectoral fins and long tail filaments, and become more aggressive.

On small reefs, each secondary male dominates and controls a harem. As he prepares to spawn, he will be so persistently aggressive to the primary males that they have to seek shelter in the reef. The secondary male then turns bright blue and, as high tide approaches, he performs loops in the water, signalling to the females that he is ready to spawn. In the mating display that follows, he swims above the reef while quivering his body and flaunting his pectoral fins. Eventually, a female will join him and they rush to the surface to release their gametes. Soon other females follow suit and he may spawn with eight or more in one day. The primary males play no part in the spawning, and so they tend to be sparse on small reefs.

Primary males fare better and so are more abundant on larger reefs where moon wrasse are more spread out. There, a secondary male still holds a territory but he does not have control over the primary males, which tend to wander more freely over the reef. As spawning approaches, several secondary males and females gather at an outcrop on the reef, and they are joined by groups of primary males. When the pairs swim up to release their gametes near the surface, many primary males join in the rush and release sperm as well. Each secondary male is overcome by the sheer numbers of primary males, and any amount of aggression cannot drive them away.

The largest hermaphrodite fish we came across were the most common reef-dwelling predators, the groupers. In Australia, groupers are commonly called cod, and the most impressive we saw were the potato cod at the world-famous site, Cod Hole. These fish are coloured light beige with darker blotches. They are simply huge, averaging about 1.5 metres (5 feet) in length and weighing 100 kilograms (220 pounds) each. When we got into the water they were just visible as big shapes swimming towards us from afar, but within a minute or so we were surrounded. Occasionally these giants rushed at each other, demonstrating that they had some sort of hierarchy which had just been violated and reminding us of their extraordinary power. Generally, though, they were relatively benign. Their low slung, very wide mouths were full of tiny backward-pointing teeth that looked more likely to cause a serious graze than to do any lasting damage. They had a curious nature and seemed to solicit strokes as well as enjoying being tickled under the chin.

Elsewhere in the world, such as in the Caribbean and certain parts of the Pacific, some groupers congregate to spawn, both in small numbers and in their thousands. As yet, no such gatherings have been seen in the Great Barrier Reef. Indeed, little is known about their reproduction there, other than that the fish in some species change from female to male.

Fish in the tropics can spawn all year round, but those on the Great Barrier Reef tend to do so during the summer when the water is warmer. At this time, too, winds and ocean currents are less strong, reducing the likelihood that the larvae in the plankton will be swept far out into the ocean with little hope of being brought back to the reef. Fish usually spawn a number of times over the summer months, thereby increasing the chances that some of their offspring will come out of the plankton just as a space on the reef becomes available.

Broadcast spawning fish tend to release their gametes on or near either the full moon or the new moon. At these times there are larger tides to wash the eggs clear of both waving tentacles and hungry mouths waiting nearby to catch them. For the same reason, the fish usually release their gametes high in the water. Many choose to spawn above coral heads or outcrops so that they can retreat into the reef quickly

ABOVE: A male fairy basslet surrounded by his harem. BELOW: Detail of the tiny *Anthias pleurotaenia*, a fairy basslet.

RIGHT: A relative of the tiny fairy basslet is the potato cod. This one was awesome – but friendly.

if danger threatens. Congregating at such spawning sites may also help fish to find willing partners more quickly.

Since broadcast spawners do not care for their young, the males of some species will try to spawn with as many females as possible, rushing from one to another. A very different strategy is adopted by others, such as certain species of butterflyfish. The identical-looking males and females of these ornately coloured fish form stable, long-term monogamous pairs and do not change sex. There are various possible benefits of forming pairs for the breeding season. These fish are well spaced out over the reef and, since they need to spawn at dusk or shortly after when their gametes will be safer, it may be that the males simply do not have time to search out a second female. Also, the eggs of fish mature over some time and monogamy allows the male to be with the female just as her eggs ripen. But the monogamous butterflyfish stay together all year round. The main clue to this behaviour is that the butterflyfish that form pairs are those that hold territories on the reef. Two butterflyfish are much more likely to retain a territory in the face of competition than a solitary fish. So monogamy seems to be a convenient way of obtaining both a secure food supply and a mate at the same time.

Courtship and spawning in butterflyfish is rarely seen for it is very brief. The only warning that spawning is about to occur is that the female's abdomen becomes swollen prior to the day. The male follows the female around, nudging her abdomen. Then, around sunset, they rise above the reef in the same formation and quickly release their gametes into the water before returning to the shelter of the reef.

The female releases about 20 000 buoyant, transparent eggs, each less than a millimetre across. Larvae hatch from the eggs about 28 hours after fertilisation, and are sustained at first by the yolk and later by eating other members of the plankton. Butterflyfish larvae take on a form quite unlike that of any other reef fish larvae. They resemble miniature, laterally compressed, silver fish, being encased in thin, transparent bony plates. The larvae spend a long time in the plankton, probably several months, and retain their bony plates even when they settle out on to the reef under cover of darkness. As adults some feed on coral, but juvenile butterflyfish often settle in places with no coral. As they mature, their diet changes and they move on to the reef, establishing their own territory.

Some fish do not broadcast their spawn into the open water but lay their eggs on the reef. These demersal spawners lay fewer eggs and invest more time in them, tending the eggs until they hatch. Their larvae are usually larger and more developed than those of broadcast spawners and so stand a better chance of surviving in the plankton. Some of the larvae are drawn to the light so that as soon as they hatch they head to the surface and away from the ensnaring tentacles of corals.

Triggerfish are demersal spawners that live in harems containing a male and several females. Each female holds a small territory, and the male's territory encompasses the whole harem. Among fish, it is usually the male or, in some cases, both sexes that tend the eggs. Female triggerfish are the only ones known to be solely responsible for the eggs, possibly because they have much smaller territories to defend than the male. In some triggerfish, the female digs a nest site in the sand and spawning occurs before dawn. The female then tends her brood, although this is a short-lived task, providing yet another reason for her to tackle it alone. Triggerfish have the shortest incubation time of any demersal spawners and the eggs hatch just 12 to 24 hours after fertilisation.

In contrast, anemone fish tend their eggs for weeks. These fish, also known as clownfish, live in sea anemones which have harpoon-like stinging cells capable of paralysing and killing other fish. Anemone fish are not harmed by the 'harpoons', indeed they do not even trigger their release. This is because the fish secrete a mucus so similar to the anemone's mucus that they are not recognised as potential prey. The fish cannot produce this mucus at first, but acquire the ability within hours or days of moving out of the plankton and on to an anemone. Some species of anemone fish can settle on only one species of anemone, while others have a choice.

Among their host's stinging tentacles, anemone fish are safe from many predators. But if they venture far from their restricted territory they may get eaten, so they cannot roam the reef in search of a mate. In addition, sea anemones are too small to support more than a very few adult fish. These could live in monogamous pairs, but then the death of a partner would be a disaster. The surviving fish would have to wait for a larva to settle out of the plankton and mature before it could reproduce. This would be a waste of valuable reproductive time. Anemone fish overcome this problem by living in groups comprising a female and several males. All members of the group are the same colour but vary in size in a stepwise progression with the largest being the dominant female. This arrangement is possible because, unusually for fish, anemone fish start their reproductive life as males and only later in life do they change into females.

Finding a niche on the reef is not an easy undertaking for a young anemone fish settling out of the plankton. Only 10 of the 800 species of anemone can be used as refuges. The juvenile fish is guided to the correct species by a chemical emanating from the anemone. Having located a potential home, the young fish has to contend

LEFT: Male moon wrasse surrounded by females.   RIGHT: Anemone fish are unaffected by these stinging tentacles.

with any resident anemone fish, all aggressive to new arrivals. If the patch is full they will chase away the newcomer and, unless it finds another suitable anemone quickly, it will be eaten by predators.

To become established, the young fish must find an anemone that has recently grown or one that has a reduced group of fish. Then the newcomer will be accepted into the group, finding itself at the bottom of the size hierarchy. The largest fish, the dominant female, keeps all the other fish in the group as either immature or subadult males by aggression. If the female dies or is eaten by a predator, her position is soon filled by the largest male. Within a day, he is aggressive to all the other males, and

within a month, 'he' is a fully functional female capable of laying eggs. Each of the other members of the group also move up a step in the hierarchy.

The only fish in the group that breed are the proven survivors – the female and the largest male. When the female is ripe, the male bites back the anemone and clears a patch of rock underneath. Enticed by him, she lays several hundred eggs and he rushes in to fertilise them. Although both partners may fan, clean and protect the eggs, the male does most of the work, just as the male garibaldi fish does in California. The eggs start off orange and gradually turn silver as the eyes of the larvae inside develop. After one to two weeks the larvae hatch out at night and swim into the plankton.

In the animal kingdom, a male does not generally waste his time and energy caring for another male's young, but anemone fish are an exception. If the father dies while the eggs are developing, the female will tend them for a short time. Then the next male in line will take over from her, and all the smaller fish will move up a step. It is apparently worth the male's while to act as stepfather in order to be accepted as her future mate.

The messmate pipefish also invests a great deal in a small number of young. This is a buff-coloured, sinuous, pencil-like fish, which grows up to 18 centimetres (7 inches) long. Each is faithful to one mate, and the males are among the few fish that carry the eggs. Whether he is carrying eggs or not, the female journeys to the male's territory every day to maintain the bond between the pair. At a greeting site the pair go through a series of movements not unlike their courtship ritual.

Courtship for the messmate pipefish occurs at dawn near the male's sleeping site and spawning follows one to three hours later. The ritual starts with the pair swimming in parallel. They arch their abdomens off the seabed, rise up vertically in the water, entwining their bodies, and the female releases her eggs into the male's now open pouch where they are fertilised. The pair then perform a 'dance' in which the male wriggles his body against hers, apparently settling the eggs in his pouch and ensuring that they stick to the pouch walls. Ten or so days later, the eggs hatch, and well-developed, free-swimming larvae emerge at dusk.

For the grey and white puller fish, parental duties are not over even when the eggs hatch. Both parents tend the eggs, the larvae and then the young fry. The tiny silvery offspring spend the day above the coral, searching for plankton with their parents, and at night are ushered back into the shelter of the reef. Since the fry are not allowed to venture far from their parents, they cannot disperse to other reefs. This means that populations in different areas seldom intermix and can become quite distinct from each other. For example, there may be colour differences between populations only 100 kilometres (60 miles) apart.

An even better way of protecting the young is to retain them within the parent until they are ready to face life on the reef as miniature adults. The largest among the reef animals that use this strategy are some sharks. The two we saw most frequently were the whitetip and grey reef sharks.

Whitetip reef sharks have, as their name implies, white tips to their dorsal fin and tail. They are so common that it is unusual to dive on the Great Barrier Reef and not see at least one of these small, slender sharks. Grey reef sharks are also easy to recognise. They are only slightly longer than the whitetips, up to 2.5 metres (8 feet) or so, but are more bulky. Both the trailing edge of their tail and the underside of their pectoral fins are black, contrasting with the grey-bronze colour over the back and the white underside. Grey reef sharks move in an erratic way, swimming slowly and smoothly and then making sudden bursts of movement, before reverting to their previous graceful motion. They also have an impressive ability to change direction almost instantaneously, which can be disconcerting when you're swimming with them.

'Grey reef sharks don't have a great reputation. They are unpredictable, twitchy and can get aggressive. But don't worry.' Those were the words quietly spoken to me on my way into the water. Together with our lack of shark suits or any other protective gear, this advice made me feel more than a little apprehensive. Once in the water, the sharks appeared reassuringly distant, cruising along the drop-off and out in the blue water beyond. It was not long, however, before the sharks became curious about us and moved in to investigate, first the whitetip reef sharks and then the grey reef sharks.

The grey reef sharks did, indeed, seem menacing as they approached. One would appear out of the blue, heading directly for us. While barely moving its tail for propulsion, it would narrow the distance between us at an alarming rate. When it was within a few feet of us it would turn sharply and I would breathe a short sigh of relief, only to look up and see another one homing in on us.

While many fish have to search for a mate, the problem is greater for sharks. Being top predators, sharks are fewer in number than most fish and have to space themselves out more in order to find enough food. So sharks have had to develop ways of ensuring that, when they do get a chance to mate, eggs will be fertilised and develop

OVERLEAF: Grey reef sharks are often seen on remote reefs. They give birth to live, fully formed young.

into offspring. All sharks use the same method to ensure that eggs will meet sperm – internal fertilisation.

As mentioned earlier, male sharks are easily identified by the pair of claspers on their underside. These are part of the modified pelvic fins and one is inserted into the female during mating. Males probably find receptive females by a combination of sight and smell. Their keen eyesight allows them to recognise another of their species at a distance. A male may use his sense of smell to ascertain the female's condition. In some species, he will follow the female closely, his nose in line with her genital opening. The male induces the female to copulate by biting her and male whitetip reef sharks continue biting the female's pectoral fin during copulation to maintain contact. Larger sharks may also do this but few have been observed mating. The bites can be quite vicious and most adult females have mating scars on their dorsal fin and along their back.

Sharks mate with their bodies parallel and their reproductive organs aligned. Whitetip reef sharks often take up a vertical position with their heads on the reef as the male inserts one of his claspers into the female. Special sacs inside his belly flood with sea water and then contract, flushing his sperm along a groove in the clasper and into his mate.

Many female sharks can store sperm, the blue sharks we saw in California, for example, being able to retain sperm for up to a year. This allows the female to mate when there is a male around, and to fertilise her eggs later, when she is ready. The females invest a great deal in relatively few fertilised eggs, and so increase the chances of each developing embryo surviving.

Sharks have evolved three ways of protecting their fertilised eggs. Some, like the horn shark in California, simply lay a leathery egg case with the embryo attached to a yolk sac inside. Other females keep their eggs within them and the embryos develop into miniature adults, sustained by the yolk. Those in the third group, such as grey reef sharks, invest the most in their young. Again, the mother retains her embryos but when they have exhausted the yolk they become attached to a placenta and are fed by the mother's blood. As a result, the young sharks are born very well developed and able to face the rigours of the ocean. Grey reef sharks give birth to at least eight pups at a time, each a hungry, 60 centimetre (24 inch) long predator.

Sharks that give birth to live young retain their embryos for up to a year. Even within the mother, the developing young are not completely safe. The growing embryos are as predatory inside the mother as they are in later life and as they develop may eat their siblings. Despite such losses, many more survive than would in the open water and the pups that do make it are relatively large and capable of hunting on their own from birth.

A further advantage of live-bearing is that the female does not have to go in search of a secure site in which to deposit her eggs, but can remain in open water and continue feeding. Another group of animals, the turtles, swim great distances from their feeding grounds to their chosen nest site. They also have to lay a large number of eggs in order that one or two may survive to adulthood.

An island at the extreme north of the Great Barrier Reef is the destination for a nesting colony of far-ranging green turtles. They are thought to return to the very same site each time they breed, some travelling over 2700 kilometres (1700 miles) to nest on one particular beach. Both the males and the females make the journey and arrive on the Great Barrier Reef in spring, between September and October. They mate frequently with many partners for some weeks and then the males leave.

Females come ashore to start laying eggs soon after they first mate. They also store sperm and will continue to come ashore every 13 days or so until they have laid all their eggs. Each female may lay as many as eight clutches in all, using the high tide to help her up the sometimes steep beach at night. She clambers up as early as possible in the night for if she is not back in the water by late morning when the sun is high, she will bake to death.

We arrived on the island in the first week of December, the peak of the turtles' nesting season. That night, they came in their hundreds, a late evening count totalling over 1250 animals. The sight of a seemingly endless stream of large animated dark objects climbing slowly and inexorably out of the water up the steep sand and on to the beach was almost sinister. Even stranger was the scene further up the beach. As we walked in the moonlight, all we could see were puffs of sand shooting into the air along the entire length of the beach. The upper part of the beach was dry, and it was there that the digging activity was concentrated, giving it a cratered appearance. After an hour or more of digging, with sand flying in all directions, each turtle has formed a pit for her body and sits well down in it. Using her hind flippers, she digs an egg chamber 25 centimetres (10 inches) wide and penetrating 50 centimetres (20 inches) deep into the wet sand, and is then ready to drop her eggs.

Until she actually starts laying, a turtle is easily disturbed and will return to the water. Once the egg-laying process begins, though, she goes into a trance-like state and from that moment on will lay her clutch despite most disturbances. So we waited quietly for this critical time and then crept closer to look at the egg-laying. We dug away the back of a chamber and saw the eggs dropping out of the female, two or

LEFT: A green turtle returns to the sea at dawn, sandy and exhausted after a night of laying eggs.
RIGHT: After about 2 months the hatchlings emerge and scramble seaward.

three at a time. This was happening all over the island during that and subsequent nights, and we were all aware of the great privilege it was to witness this event.

A female may lay between 60 and 150 eggs at a time, a typical clutch size being 110. This only takes about 10 minutes, and then she starts filling in the chamber and the pit. By the time she has finished shifting sand, the exact position of the eggs is well disguised and she is exhausted. She recovers for some while before heading back to the water, where she stays, fasting, for about 13 days. Then she comes ashore again to dig another nest. By the end of the season she will have laid between 500 and 1000 eggs, of which only one or two will reach adulthood.

The newly laid eggs are like soft ping-pong balls, their softness preventing damage

as they fall on top of each other. Within a few days the shells' surface moisture has been absorbed and they have developed into tough, protective cases. Little threatens the encased, buried embryos apart from the odd crab. They are incubated by the warmth of the sand for 8–11 weeks, depending on the weather. Strangely, the sex of the hatchlings is not fixed at fertilisation but is determined later by the temperature of the sand. Warmer sand produces a clutch of females, while cooler sand results in males. No one is quite sure why this should be so.

Most hatchlings emerge from their sandy chamber under the cover of darkness and head towards the brightest horizon, which tends to be the light-reflecting sea. Almost all these tiny turtles, with shells only about 4 centimetres (1.5 inches) long, will make it to the water, but from then on the depredation is enormous. Night herons stand in wait on the reef flat and numerous sharks patrol the shallows near nesting beaches. Any turtles that emerge late, at dawn, stand even less chance of survival with seabirds and many more reef predators awake.

The very few young that manage to clear the reef flat swim out to sea, sustained by the remains of yolk sac that they ingest just before hatching. Where these tiny turtles spend their first years is a mystery, but for some time they may drift in ocean currents, feeding on plankton. When they reappear in shallow water feeding on algae, they are 10–15 years old and about 35 centimetres (14 inches) long. Every year or two they move on to a new feeding area until they are fully mature at about 40 to 50 years of age. Only then do they migrate back to the beach where they were born, to nest for the first time.

Even adult turtles are threatened by predators, including groupers and sharks and, the most effective of all, man. Of seven species of turtle, six are endangered or threatened purely as a result of human activities. For example, the green turtle is sought for its skin to make leather, its oil for cosmetics, its scales for jewellery and ornaments, and its offal for fertiliser. Most prized of all is the green flesh from which it gets its name. This is used to make turtle soup, a prized delicacy in many parts of the world. In the 1920s, there was a boom in demand for turtle products and over 1000 green turtles were slaughtered on the Great Barrier Reef each year. By 1950, the grave effects of this destruction on turtle populations were obvious and the green turtle was protected by Australian law. But turtles cross international boundaries while most laws do not. Although it is an international problem, individuals have a responsibility and can help by refusing to buy turtle products of any description.

A much smaller animal than man is capable of posing a less direct but just as serious threat to life in and around the reefs. The crown of thorns starfish kills live coral and, when its populations explode, can destroy an entire reef. This bizarre looking creature is sinister, repulsive, intriguing and beautiful at the same time. It is one of the world's largest starfish, averaging 30 centimetres (12 inches) from arm tip to arm tip, although some individuals grow as big as 70 centimetres (28 inches). The number of arms varies from 6 to 23, each bristling with toxic spines tipped with three raised cutting edges. The starfish's colouring varies through a range from purple with red spines to green with yellow spines.

I received an unparalleled view of the underside of one of these creatures when it was placed on my bubble helmet by another diver. The hundreds of yellow-suckered tube feet, huge for a starfish, worked their way across the dome. The tube feet are common to all echinoderms (starfish, sea urchins and the like) and run in rows from the central mouth to the ends of each arm. They can be used to cling on to surfaces, to move, in sensing the surroundings and in feeding. They are controlled by a complex hydraulic system consisting of valves, muscular sacs, tubes and reservoirs.

The stomach was also clearly visible as a yellow membranous mass in the centre of the disc. When the starfish feeds, it turns the stomach inside out and spreads it over the coral using its tube feet. Digestive enzymes then get to work and break down the living tissues of the coral, including the wax where energy is stored. When the starfish withdraws its stomach, all that remains of the coral is the white skeleton.

The crown of thorns starfish has a preference for certain corals, usually the ones with small polyps. One starfish will take four to six hours to eat an area of coral the size of a small plate but, since it does this daily, an individual starfish can eat over 5 square metres (54 square feet) of coral in a year. Corals may be immobile and unable to retreat from the threat, but the species with larger polyps do put up a fight. The stinging cells are particularly nasty around the edges of corals and are fired at the encroaching predator. If this does not deter the starfish, crabs and shrimps living within the coral's branches may come to its aid. These tiny crustaceans pinch the underside of the starfish until it retreats. The lovely Christmas tree worms, found embedded in or around the coral head, can also irritate the predator to such an extent that it moves on. Other corals produce copious amounts of mucus, making it difficult for the starfish to secure a hold.

Having the starfish on my bubble helmet meant that I could not see anything beyond, and nor could I reach the helmet's flush button to give myself a breath of fresh air without touching the animal's inch-long spines. The hundreds of spines are covered with tissue containing an irritant-poison that can produce serious allergic reactions in people, the worst case reported to date having resulted in amputation of the victim's leg. Fortunately, the starfish moved of its own accord and I could see and breathe freely again.

The spines also deter most would-be predators, but a few animals have overcome the defence. Some emperor fish may feed on smaller, more vulnerable crown of thorns starfish, and large pufferfish and triggerfish can overturn an adult to attack its vulnerable underside. The giant triton shell, a large and beautiful snail, holds on to the starfish, cuts it open with its saw-like mouth parts and sucks out the flesh.

Watching a female crown of thorns spawning showed us how amply such losses to predators could be replaced. Literally millions upon millions of eggs, looking rather like red sand grains, streamed out of tiny pores in her thorny disc. Surprisingly,

LEFT: An unusual view of the crown of thorns starfish – not a hat for Ascot!

RIGHT: My view of the starfish – its seldom seen tube feet.

the eggs were not very buoyant and dropped down between her arms on to the reef. Like the giant clam, this starfish synchronises spawning by releasing chemical messages with the gametes.

Each fertilised egg hatches after a day into a larva that feeds on microscopic algae in the plankton and swims by beating hairs. The eggs and larvae contain unpalatable substances called saponins, which may be the reason why relatively few seem to be eaten by fish. After three to four weeks the larva's hind part has developed into an embryonic starfish and it settles out of the plankton on to the reef. A couple of days later it has absorbed the front part and is recognisably a starfish, although only 0.5 millimetre (0.02 inch) across. At this stage, ironically, it is susceptible to being eaten by coral polyps and survives by feeding on encrusting algae. When it is six months old and about the size of a penny, it is able to switch to feeding on coral and starts to grow very quickly. Even then it is threatened by many predators and has to hide under rocks and in crevices on the reef, only emerging at night to feed. At two years old, the starfish is about 14 centimetres (5.5 inches) across and is sexually mature.

A low population of crown of thorns starfish can be sustained by a reef and may actually enhance the diversity of corals. By selectively eating the most abundant and fastest growing species, the starfish clear areas for colonisation by the slower, less plentiful corals. Many reefs have a small resident population of these starfish, which are difficult to see because they hide in the day and only feed at night. When populations are large, though, the starfish are forced to feed both day and night and are easily spotted.

Each female releases 20 million eggs during the summer spawning. Normally, all but a few of these are lost through low success in fertilisation, shortage of algae in the water for the larvae, and predators. But if conditions are very favourable, the success rate can increase dramatically. For example, crown of thorns starfish prefer an area with not too much turbulence, not too much sand and the right variety of coral. Once they move into such an area and start to feed on the coral, chemicals released in the feeding process attract other crown of thorns starfish. If this gathering of adults spawns, many eggs will be successfully fertilised. A good supply of algae in the water will allow many to survive the larval stage. Furthermore, the larvae that settle on the parent reef will find recently killed coral heads with no polyps to eat them. If, in these and other ways, just 0.01 per cent of one female's eggs survive to adulthood, there will be an additional 2000 starfish on the reef.

Huge outbreaks of the crown of thorns do occur from time to time on the Great Barrier Reef, and such infestations cause extensive damage to the coral on a reef. Once a reef is depleted of the preferred corals, the starfish may move to another reef. Alternatively, they may start eating other corals, sea urchins, clams and algae, or they may simply fast for a number of months. Their adaptability renders them a persistent menace.

Infestations were first noticed on the Great Barrier Reef in 1962 and controversy over the causes has raged ever since. Some think that the population explosions have been brought about by man's activities. One suggested cause is the reduction of the starfish's predators through, for example, the collection of giant tritons for their shells and the fishing of emperor bream. This seems unlikely because triton numbers are naturally low, even on inaccessible reefs, and each eats at most only one starfish a day. Emperor bream, triggerfish and pufferfish may all eat starfish, but seldom feed extensively on them. A more plausible argument is that the run-off from agricultural lands increases nutrient levels in the water and so nourishes the algae on which starfish larvae depend.

The death of corals on a reef is of great concern to those in the tourist industry. It is considerably worse for fish, such as some species of butterflyfish, that depend solely on living coral polyps for food. Reefs that have suffered from crown of thorns outbreaks may have significantly reduced numbers of such fish. In a campaign to solve the infestation problem, divers tried to clear the reef of starfish but this proved ineffectual, time consuming and exorbitantly expensive. While a bacteria that can kill as much as 99 per cent of a juvenile starfish population is being investigated, it is hoped that such a drastic solution will never need to be used.

The infestations are not continuous but cyclical. For example, when an infestation has destroyed a reef, the starfish eventually die off and the reef will probably regenerate in 5 to 15 years before the next infestation. Fossilised remains of the starfish's spines show that the crown of thorns has been a reef inhabitant for over 8000 years. These points suggest to some that the infestations are natural, have always occurred and need no unnatural, and possibly devastating, controls from outside the reef ecosystem. If this is the case, human activities on and around the reef will still need to be curbed so that we do not upset the natural balance.

Whatever their cause, the infestations will be carefully monitored for the reefs lie within the Great Barrier Reef Marine Park, the largest protected marine area in the world. This is divided into zones for fishing, for education, for recreation and for scientific research. It is hoped that through such careful and considered usage, the life that depends on this, the greatest structure built by any of Earth's creatures, will be able to continue to thrive and reproduce.

THE CARIBBEAN SEA

We are as near to heaven by sea as by land.
Sir Humphrey Gilbert.

Clearing customs in Miami was, for a change, quite quick. A long wait for the connecting flight tried our patience, but the thought of what lay before us kept our spirits high. We were en route to our first location in the Atlantic, which would reveal a whole new underwater world.

The Caribbean Sea and the surrounding tropical western Atlantic are now separated from the Indo-Pacific region, which comprises the connected Indian and Pacific Oceans. At one time these waters shared common plants and animals, including corals, linked as they were by tracts of ocean. One massive ocean, the Tethys Sea, separated northern Europe and Asia from the African and Indian continents. Then, about 25 million years ago, the gap closed, and animals in the Atlantic were isolated by a land barrier to the east and a vast water barrier, the Pacific Ocean, to the west. In isolation and with environmental changes such as the rerouting of surface currents, life in the tropical Atlantic was unable to flourish to the same degree as in the Indo-Pacific. The partial deprivation in the Atlantic lasted for 10–15 million years until another barrier

Despite increasing pressure of tourism in the Caribbean, quiet beaches can still be found.

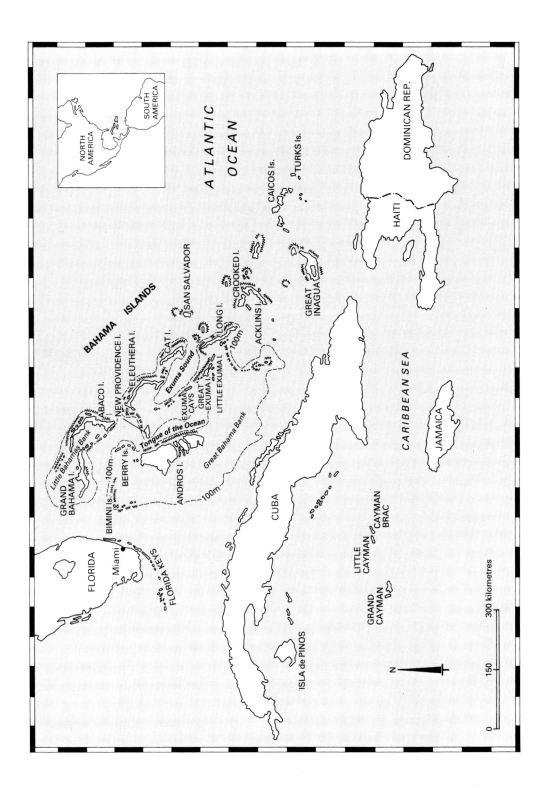

began to emerge, the Isthmus of Panama. Gradually, the number of creatures moving between the oceans decreased until 3–3.5 million years ago, when the Americas joined to become one land mass. The isolation of the tropical Atlantic, with its relative paucity of species, was then even greater.

The reefs of the Caribbean were hemmed in by the Americas to the west, cold water to the north and south, and by the water barrier of the Atlantic Ocean. As in the Great Barrier Reef, the corals of the Caribbean suffered during each period of glaciation in the Ice Ages, and today's reefs represent only 5000 years of continuous growth. Isolated for millions of years, the corals of the Caribbean have developed distinct differences from those of the Indo-Pacific. Out of a total of 100 genera, only eight are shared, and there is only one species of reef-building coral common to both regions. Also, the Caribbean has only about half the number of corals of the Indo-Pacific. This is probably due to its short evolutionary history, environmental changes and the relatively limited range of habitats it offers.

Despite the paucity of coral species, the reefs that have developed in the Caribbean are spectacular, characterised by a profusion of brightly coloured sponges, large bushy soft corals and sea fans. It is home to 90 endemic hard corals and approximately 430 species of reef fish. Although the reef life in the Caribbean has developed along separate lines from that in the Indo-Pacific, its evolution has in many instances been in parallel. So related corals and fish from the two regions fulfil similar roles.

The communities of both the Caribbean and the Indo-Pacific coral reefs are delicately balanced, and would suffer if species could move from one to the other. In 1914 the Panama Canal was completed, allowing passage of ships from one ocean to the other via a series of ascending and descending giant locks. Fortunately, a fresh-water barrier in the middle of the canal, Gatun Lake, protects both oceans by preventing the passage of marine life between them. As each of the 12 000 ships per year pass through the canal, 200 million litres (44 million gallons) of freshwater flow out to sea. This water should be replaced by rain falling on the mountain slopes that border the canal. But with increasing deforestation, the run-off is no longer slowed by trees, the surrounding lakes become low during periods of drought and the canal is drying up. Also, the removal of trees has exposed the mountain slopes to erosion and soil from them is being washed down, silting up the lakes and, in turn, the canal. So the canal is becoming too shallow for the many large supertankers that now need

OVERLEAF, LEFT: Elkhorn coral typifies shallow water reefs in the Caribbean where it grows in profusion. RIGHT: The Caribbean is noted for its sponges. This yellow tube sponge is thought to contain fluorescent pigments.

to cross the Isthmus, and alternatives are being proposed. One is a road and rail link and another is a deepening and widening of the existing canal. A third proposal, the only one backed by the US and Japan, is the construction of a sea-level waterway. While this would alleviate the problem for shipping, it would be a catastrophe for marine life.

Species would move both ways along such a canal, but the greater flow would be to the Caribbean because the Pacific has larger tides and is, on average, 30 centimetres (12 inches) higher. New diseases and predators, and competition from alien species would all threaten the Caribbean's endemic life and the equilibrium of its reefs. Foreign marine species could have as dramatic an effect on the reefs as alien land mammals have had on isolated land masses, such as rabbits in Australia or dogs and goats in the Galápagos Islands. For example, the crown of thorns starfish does not yet occur on Caribbean reefs and the corals there may have no defence against this formidable predator. Perhaps of more immediate concern to most people, poisonous sea snakes that live in open water in the Pacific would invade the Caribbean. Hopefully a realisation of the degeneration that would occur will deter a new breach of the Isthmus, and the unique life we encountered in the Caribbean will continue to thrive in isolation.

We spent part of our time around the Bahama Islands in the tropical western Atlantic. Although they lie to the north of the Caribbean Sea, the Bahamian reefs house animals similar to those in the slightly warmer southern waters. This is because their western edge is bathed by the Florida Current of the Gulf Stream which brings warm water and the larvae of animals living on reefs in the south. The Bahamas stretch from Florida in the north to Cuba and Haiti in the south and offer 2750 islands, cays and rocks for animals to colonise. These islands are the exposed tips of two large submarine plateaux, the Great and Little Bahama Banks, which are only 5–20 metres (16–65 feet) deep. Both banks have a similar structure: the largest islands occur along the north and east edges of the plateaux, the central parts are flat and shallow, while only low islands and rocks are found along the south and west edges. The Great Bahama Bank is almost split by a deep chasm called the Tongue of the Ocean on one side and by Exuma Sound on the other.

The Bahamian area is of great geological interest for it is one of the few places where lime (calcium carbonate) is being deposited in warm shallow seas, a process which was common in times past. The banks are made of nearly pure calcium carbonate, and extensive cavern complexes in the limestone reach the surface both inland and at sea, giving rise to what are popularly called the Blue Holes. Throughout the Bahamas, fringing reefs grow along the edges of the islands. Those in the east suffer the full impact of the Atlantic Ocean, while in the rest of the Bahamas reef growth may be limited by low winter temperatures and storms.

We also explored the waters around the Caymans. The three Cayman Islands, Grand Cayman, Little Cayman and Cayman Brac, are true Caribbean islands, protected from the Atlantic by the Greater Antilles. They are situated in the middle of a circle that can be drawn through Cuba, the Yucatan peninsula, Honduras and Jamaica. Although also made of limestone, their origin is very different from that of the Bahamas. A fault stretches from Puerto Rico in the east to beyond Guatemala in the west, and passes near the Caymans as a deep trench called the Cayman Trench. Its northern edge is the towering Cayman Ridge, and the peaks of three of the mountains rising from this form the surprisingly flat Cayman Islands. Other mountains along the ridge fall just short of the surface. One such reef lying to the west of Grand Cayman is Twelve Mile Bank, its summit only 20 metres (65 feet) deep.

The drop on either side of the Caymans is spectacularly sheer. To the south the Cayman Trench boasts the deepest point in the Caribbean at 8400 metres (27 500 feet), while to the north the Ridge drops away sharply into the Yucatan Basin. The water around the Caymans is also very clear because the limestone of the islands and their mangrove swamps filter any rainwater. This process is aided by the flatness of the islands which are only 20 metres (65 feet) at their highest point. Rainwater percolates down through the limestone rather than running off the surface and so there are no sediment-bearing streams to cloud the oceanic water.

The combination of steep walls and clear water has made the Cayman Islands famous among scuba divers, and these attributes are even better appreciated at extreme depth. The only way to venture really deep is in a submersible, such as the one operating off Grand Cayman which we used to explore the Cayman Trench. We took the inflatable out to the waiting submersible and lowered ourselves down into the tight confines of its interior. Excited but apprehensive, I waited in the convex dome for the hatch to be sealed and within minutes we were dropping away from the surface, down on to the reef. As we descended, the submersible groaned and creaked under the increasing water pressure, the ballast shifted, and the hum of the engines soon sank to a reassuring background murmur. I was transfixed by the changing scenery outside. From about 50 metres (165 feet), the wall drops down

OVERLEAF, LEFT: Fragile sea fans grow at right angles to the current to enhance the capture of food from the water.
RIGHT: Christmas tree worms – food is collected by the beating of fine hairs on the spiral whorls.

almost vertically into the trench. The wall is not smooth but rugged, and has spurs which create irregular folds in its face and steep gullies which channel sediment to the floor below. The vast expanse of plummeting cliffs and massive overhangs made the submersible seem very insignificant and vulnerable.

At this depth too, the corals typical of the shallow reefs were becoming rare, and where they did grow they tended to be thin and encrusting, disappearing completely by about 80 metres (260 feet). Very soon we were entering the 'sponge zone', a belt along the wall that stretches to 200 metres (650 feet) deep and houses the most fantastic array of brilliantly coloured sponges.

Sponges grow more prolifically in Caribbean waters than they do in the Indo-Pacific, and are most profuse in the Caymans, which are often called the sponge capital of the world. Over 30 varieties of sponges are found there, inhabiting many areas of the reef. Some are largely hidden in the reef because they bore into the coral, dissolving its calcium carbonate skeleton. As more of these boring sponges make room for themselves, the coral crumbles and eventually disintegrates. Other sponges grow on the surface of the reef. Those that inhabit shallow waters are often rounded and flattened against the reef. Sponges in shallow water may become smothered by algae, for, unlike corals, they have no mucus to deter encroaching algae. Once the algae have smothered the sponge's pores, it dies. Some find safety from algae and exposure on the reef crest by growing in caves and under overhangs. In deeper water, sheltered from the sometimes rough seas above, the sponges can grow to enormous proportions and take on a wide variety of shapes. On the vertical walls were 3 metre (10 foot) wide giant orange elephant ear sponges, tube sponges of vivid purple, and rope sponges of orange, red or yellow dripping off overhangs and cascading down the cliff face.

A sponge is an assemblage or colony of self-contained cells that function as a whole. If a fragment of the colony is broken off, the cells in it can generate an entirely new sponge. The skeleton of a sponge is made up of interlocked needle-like spicules of silicon or calcium carbonate, with a network of spongy fibres known as spongin. The spicules are so fine that it is difficult to feel them, and unwary divers who rub their hands along sponges, or just touch them, get covered in spicules without even realising it. They can cause severe irritation and some are very painful.

Like corals, many Indo-Pacific sponges have microscopic algae living within them that manufacture food for them. Few Caribbean sponges do, and instead they have to obtain their food by filtering the water. An average-sized sponge gains the food and oxygen it needs by filtering approximately 2000 litres (440 gallons) of water every 24 hours. Each sponge has minute holes all over its surface, and whip-like appendages on the sponge's cells generate currents that draw water through the holes. The sponge is an efficient filterer and can remove particles down to only one thousandth of a millimetre in size. The waste products are washed out by water that leaves the sponge through holes which are visible to the human eye and, in the large sponges, through a central cavity. By taking out minute particles sponges improve the clarity of the water substantially.

Below the level of the sponges, at 240 metres (790 feet), we entered an area of giant boulders. It was easy to misjudge size and distance through the convex port, and what had appeared to be cracks in the wall developed into canyons as we approached. Similarly, the boulders that had appeared to be merely quite large began to tower above us. The 30 metre (100 foot) tall boulders, or haystacks as they are called, are thought to have broken off and fallen from the cliff face. When we turned off the lights I was surprised that the ambient light, although dim, allowed us to see boulders over 100 metres (330 feet) away. With no land mass nearby, and nutrient poor water limiting phytoplankton growth, the water contains very few clouding particles to block out light from above.

Further down, at 300 metres (1000 feet), the scene was much darker and very eerie, reminiscent of a still, moonlit night. There was little colour down here, because without light, colours become redundant. The starkness of this monochromatic vista was further emphasised by the existence of a white blanket of sediment that lay over the seabed and dusted the tops of rocks. This sediment is made up of plankton, detritus and sediment and the few animals living at such depths depend on this 'marine snow' for food.

The stillness of the scene was due to the almost total absence of roving animals. With too little light for plants to survive, there is, in turn, a dearth of animals, except for some specially adapted species. The few corals that snare the food drifting by in the gentle current look completely different from those living above. For example, the extremely brittle porcelain coral looks more like an intricate, china white, lace fan than a colony of living polyps. Perhaps the strangest inhabitant is an echinoderm, a relative of starfish and sea urchins. The Great West Indian sea lily has barely changed in 230 million years, as virtually identical fossils of that age show. It grows on a stalk up to 60 centimetres (2 feet) tall, and hangs on to the rock with claw-like hooks. Opening from the stalk, an elegant whorl of 60 or more arms filter passing food particles from the water. Sea lilies appear immobile but they can move at a

OVERLEAF: The arms of this nocturnal shallow-water sea lily curl gracefully as it feeds.

painfully slow pace, imperceptible to us. To do so, they release their grasp on the rock, lie down and use their arms to crawl along the bottom.

It was with great regret that I felt the submersible start on its upward journey. We paused for one last look at the ghostly panorama of this lunar seascape, and then ascended slowly past the changing habitats of the wall. The frenetic activity and kaleidoscopic colours of the shallow reefs jarred on us after the tranquillity of the abyss.

The shallow shelf that surrounds Grand Cayman is 0.5–2 kilometres (0.3–1.2 miles) wide, and rises in a series of small terraces from the walls below. Within the shallow fringing reefs encircling the islands lie sandy lagoons and it was these we explored next. I viewed this location with some trepidation knowing that, in one of the lagoons, southern stingrays occur in their dozens. When I was four or five years old, the one animal that could prevent me from swimming out to sea was the stingray, and this unreasoning fear still lingered.

We started off without diving or snorkelling equipment, awaiting the stingrays in waist-deep water wearing no more than our swimming costumes. Having been assured they would not hurt me, I made an effort to feel confident and took a deep breath. Then a squadron of black shapes approached swiftly through the shallows. The stingrays were huge, 1.5 metres (5 feet) or so across with a long, whip-like tail, and swam around our legs in an unnervingly familiar way. Soon the water between us was filled with a constant whirl of stingray. While knowing I should keep still, I automatically tried to step out of their way, only to find there was simply no bare sand where I could put down my raised leg. It was while I was unbalanced, with one leg precariously outstretched, that I felt, not a sting, but a sharp bite, and left the water in an inelegant hurry.

Like sharks and other rays, stingrays have no bones and are instead supported by cartilage. They have a very flattened body and this, together with their head and enlarged pectoral fins, forms a disc. The animal propels itself by sinuous undulations of the disc edge. Southern stingrays usually feed on molluscs, worms and crustaceans living in the sand. At other times they can be found simply resting, themselves buried in the sand, exposing just their eyes which are located on top of their head. They have enlarged holes, or spiracles, behind the eyes through which they take in water. They breathe by pumping this water over the gills, which extract oxygen, and expelling it through the gill slits located on the underside.

When threatened the stingray will whip up its long, thin tail which bears, on its upper edge, a poisonous spine. This has saw-toothed edges and grooves running along each side and it is these which contain the poison. It was the spine that I had always been afraid of, although people are usually only wounded when they unwarily tread on a stingray buried in the sand. Those unfortunate enough to do so may experience swelling and fever accompanied by extreme pain and, in a very few severe cases, can die.

When we returned to the water fully kitted up, I felt completely at ease with the rays. Again they approached in perfect formation, cruising across the white sand from afar. They swam unerringly into us, gliding over our bodies, and then turned and brushed past again and again. Stingrays have a dark back and creamy white underside, and the contrast in the texture of their skin on each side was just as sharp. The upperside is protected and toughened by small tooth-like projections in the skin called denticles. It felt rather like fine-grained sandpaper dotted with small, sharp bumps. The white underside, on the other hand, was fantastically smooth and silky, reminding me of the spongy flesh of giant clam mantles. I banished my fear by stroking them as they swam by and letting my hand run down the tail and over the dreaded spine. I also let them have a go at my hand and found that their 'bite' is actually more like fierce suck. I came away with somewhat grazed fingers, for they have rows and rows of tiny blunt teeth that form hard pavements, ideal for crushing their hard-shelled prey once it has been sucked from the seabed.

Stingrays forage by digging craters in the sand and so the eyes, on top of the head, are redundant during feeding. Instead, they locate their prey using electroreceptors dotted along the front edge of the disc. Electroreceptors are found in both sharks and rays, and are thought to be used in navigation as well as prey detection. Recent evidence suggests that these animals can sense the small electric fields created by ocean currents as they move across the Earth's magnetic field. Sharks and rays probably use this inbuilt electromagnetic compass to find their way when travelling across vast tracts of featureless ocean.

Among the other predators that hunt for food in the sand of the lagoons are the triggerfish. These fish are deep-bodied, almost diamond-shaped from side on, and can grow up to 60 centimetres (24 inches) or so long. Some species are adorned with the most brilliant array of colours, particularly those of the Pacific. The most decorative Caribbean species is the queen triggerfish, which sports a bluey green back, yellowish chin and underside, two curved bright bands running back from the

OVERLEAF: What surprised me most about the southern stingrays was the texture of their skin. The creamy softness of the underside contrasts with the rough silk of the back.

snout that look rather like war paint, and dark blue lines with yellow edges radiating out from the eye. The name triggerfish comes from a modification of the spines on the dorsal fin. The front spine can be erected and then locked in position by another, smaller 'trigger' spine lying behind it. When danger threatens, the fish will seek refuge in a crevice and lock itself in so firmly that it cannot be forcibly removed.

Triggerfish are adept at dealing with prey hidden in the sand. They blow water at the sand to uncover buried crustaceans or molluscs, forming small hollows as they do so. Sharp, chisel-like teeth easily deal with the hard shells of their prey. Sea urchins are another favourite food item, and these are blown over to expose the vulnerable underside. Triggerfish also go in for larger scale excavation, and will remove sizeable pieces of rubble to uncover secretive prey. They are often followed by scavenging fish, such as goatfish, which will readily take advantage of the less conspicuous but, nevertheless, exposed animals.

Seaward of the sand-filled lagoons lies the reef proper, where fish in their thousands swim over the coral in search of food. Competition for food and space is so intense that activity continues 24 hours a day with animals working 'shifts'. Each animal has adapted to feed at a particular time and in a particular way on a certain food or foods.

At the very bottom of most of the reef's food chains are algae, making food in the sunlight by photosynthesis. Algae are the marine equivalent of grass, and without them even the corals would not exist in their present form. There are three sources of algae on the reef. Some microscopic algae float free in the water as phytoplankton. Other tiny algae live within coral polyps and some molluscs, such as the giant clam. There are also algal mats and seaweeds growing on dead coral, rocks, indeed almost anywhere there is sunlight. All these sources are exploited by the plant-eaters or herbivores of the reef.

Many of the reef fish that are active during the day, such as the parrotfish, are herbivores. Parrotfish get their name from their beak-like mouth formed from fused teeth. Armed with this tool they can forage efficiently, scraping very low-growing algae off the dead coral and rocks. They also bite or scrape live coral to get at the algae within, leaving tell-tale scars among the remaining polyps. Whether ingesting algae from living or dead coral, they tend to take in chunks of the hard skeleton with it. Similarly, parrotfish may feed on seagrasses, and when they do so they ingest sand with the plant. They grind up the coral into sand using flattened molar-like teeth that form two plates in their throat, often called the pharyngeal mill. The mechanical abrasion of the sand is thought to assist in the breakdown of the otherwise rather tough plant material. They then excrete the ground-up coral, and parrotfish voiding curtains of sand as they swim along are common sights on the reef. By their ingestion and subsequent pulverisation of coral, parrotfish contribute significantly to the erosion of a coral reef. Indeed, on protected reefs where there is little wave or storm damage, parrotfish are probably the major agents of reef erosion.

Parrotfish may gather in schools or live alone. Caribbean parrotfish are often brilliant green or blue with markings in a range of additional colours from yellow to red and purple. The various species are all quite similar in shape, and so early naturalists used the differences in colour to divide the fish into many species. Relatively recently it has been found that there are really far fewer species, each with a number of colour varieties arising from sex changes. These are as common among Caribbean reef fish as in those on the Great Barrier Reef, and many parrotfish start life as female and may later change to become male. But, like the moon wrasse, some parrotfish may start life as males (primary males) with female colours, making identification even more confusing.

When chased, some parrotfish will make for a particular cave or hole in the reef. They will also spend their nights in their chosen refuge, hidden from predators. Once in their hole, some species make themselves even more predator proof by creating a mucous cocoon around them. Glands in the skin produce copious quantities of a transparent mucus that totally encompasses the fish except for a hole at the front through which it breathes. The cocoon is thought to prevent nocturnal predators that hunt by smell, such as the moray eel, from being able to detect the sleeping parrotfish.

Parrotfish sometimes form small mixed schools with surgeonfish, another group of algae-eaters. Surgeonfish maintain territories on the reef and can live a solitary existence. At other times they terrorise the reef in vast hordes, and any fish that attempt to defend their carefully farmed crops of algae against these schools will do so in vain.

Surgeonfish are deep-bodied, narrow animals with large dorsal and anal fins that extend virtually right around the body. Also known as doctorfish or tangs, they get their names from a scalpel-like bony keel located at the base of the tail fin. The blade is folded into a horizontal groove most of the time. When it is raised, a quick sideswipe from the tail can cause serious injury to any intruder. The effectiveness of this weapon means that territorial conflicts between surgeonfish tend to be ritualised

OVERLEAF: The queen triggerfish is adept at dealing with the hard-shelled prey it uncovers from the sand.

and brief, with little harm done to the combatants. Surgeonfish occur in a variety of colours, some dull and others bright, but they all have the ability to change colour according to their mood, darkening or blanching depending on the stimulus. Invariably the blade is well outlined in a contrasting colour. For example, the blue tang, found in Caribbean waters, is a rich velvety blue with its blade picked out in yellow or white.

The wrasse family fill a wider variety of niches than surgeonfish or parrotfish. While some are very small, such as the cleaner wrasse, others reach about 2.5 metres (8 feet) or so in length, and their diets vary accordingly. Many wrasse have strong, prominent front teeth, ideal for pulling clinging molluscs off rocks or for cracking hard-shelled prey. Most eat small crabs, sea urchins, molluscs, worms and brittlestars. The smaller species feed primarily on planktonic animals, small crustaceans living amongst the coral or, as in the cleaner wrasse, on parasites of other fish.

Wrasse of the Caribbean do not compare in size with the enormous 2 metre (6.6 feet) long humphead wrasse of the Indo-Pacific, the largest Caribbean species being the Spanish hogfish, which attains a length of only 1 metre (3.3 feet) or so. Wrasse tend to be bullet-shaped and many are gaudily coloured, such as the slippery dick, one of the most frequently seen fish of the family. The male of this species has a bright green back fading to a greeny yellow below, with two purple stripes along each side, and red lines on its head and tail.

Wrasse are closely related to parrotfish and are similar to them in a number of ways. They too have pharyngeal plates which crush food before it is digested. Some species of wrasse also use the complicated reproduction system of changing sex and having two different types of male and a number of intermediate colour phases. Also, like parrotfish, wrasse are well protected at night, although very few of them nestle within mucous cocoons. Most bury themselves in the sand, or at least hide under a rock and try to cover themselves with sand.

Innumerable little damselfish hover above the reef in their search for plankton. Lining the reef crest and slope they provide a riot of colour. A particularly common damselfish in the Caribbean is the blue chromis, a small fish of an almost iridescent blue colour. It is usually seen in shimmering groups in which each fish forages alone yet gains a degree of protection from the school. These damselfish are cautious whilst feeding because they have to venture high up the water column, away from the safety of the reef, in search of their prey. They catch individual tiny animals, mainly microscopic crustaceans called copepods that abound in the plankton. When threatened these fish retreat to the reef, hiding among the branching coral. Plankton eaters, such as the damselfish, play an important part in the life of the reef. By eating the minute free-swimming animals in the water column, they trap nutrients that might otherwise be lost to the reef. When the fish defecate or die, the nutrients are transported on to the reef and in this way provide food for corals and other invertebrates. The plankton eaters themselves provide food for predators higher up the food chain.

Particular favourites of mine among the daytime reef fish are the butterflyfish. The Caribbean has only five species of butterflyfish that are commonly seen, one of which is the longsnout butterflyfish. This fish has a particularly prolonged, thin snout, which allows it to get at tiny crustaceans, worms and eggs hidden in even the smallest cracks and holes on the reef.

Many species of butterflyfish feed on coral polyps, for which their pointed snouts are ideally suited. When they ingest a polyp, they also ingest the algae living within it. Butterflyfish do not have the pharyngeal mill found in parrotfish and wrasse, so their food is not well ground up. Recently it has been found that the microscopic algae pass through the gut of butterflyfish unharmed – possibly even nourished by the nutrients in the gut – and are still alive and able to photosynthesise when they are distributed over the reef in the fish's faeces. In this way, butterflyfish may help new corals to become established, for the larvae of corals do not have their own crop of the vital algae when they settle on the reef. They may acquire them by consuming organic matter from the butterflyfish's faecal pellets, or the algae, which are mobile, may locate the corals themselves.

Longsnouts and other Caribbean butterflyfish are usually found in pairs or alone, although some species do congregate occasionally on the edge of the reef. Most Caribbean butterflyfish hold territories on the reef and, like some of the territorial butterflyfish of the Great Barrier Reef, form monogamous pairs. One species in which I have been particularly interested for a number of years, the four-eye butterflyfish, is often seen in pairs. This distinctive fish is mostly silvery yellow, with diagonal thin black lines running across its sides. It gets its name from the large black spots, one on either side near the tail, that resemble an extra pair of eyes.

Four-eye butterflyfish usually defend their territory just by swimming around the boundary to advertise their presence and demonstrate ownership of the patch, rarely needing to show aggression. They sometimes engage in ritualised conflicts, such as

OVERLEAF *(main picture)*: The blue tang, a surgeonfish, gets its name from the yellow scalpel-like blade near its tail.
OVERLEAF *(insert)*: This very young blue tang has only just begun to acquire traces of its eventual coloration.

parallel swimming or short chases, but I have never seen them head butting, the most serious expression of aggression in butterflyfish. The size of their territory tends to be inversely proportional to the available food, being smaller in areas with plenty of food. A large four-eye butterflyfish with a mate will often tolerate small members of the species within its territory. The advantage of these juveniles seems to be that they help in defence, again by advertisement rather than aggression.

Closely related to the butterflyfish are the larger and equally decorative angelfish. Apart from size the most obvious difference between these groups is that angelfish have a spine projecting backwards from each gill cover while butterflyfish do not. Large angelfish are quite common on the reef because they feed on sponges, which grow there in profusion. The Caribbean has seven species of angelfish, all endemic and ranging in size from 10 centimetres (4 inches) to about 50 centimetres (20 inches). They are territorial fish and the larger species are rather inquisitive. When underwater, we often turned to see a grey or French angelfish unobtrusively watching our movements. Most spectacular in its coloration is the less common queen angelfish and we were lucky enough to come across several of these. The adult's body is bright blue with yellow rims to each scale, and its fins are mainly yellow, the long dorsal and anal fins edged with electric blue. The face and cheeks bear blue, green and yellow patches. A ring of blue on the forehead circling a black spot flecked with blue is the 'crown' from which the fish gets its name.

Angelfish and all the other fish that feed in the day have to be continuously on the alert for signs of larger predators. These, in their turn, have had to develop clever strategies in order to catch their vigilant prey. Some, such as the scorpionfish, are coloured so that they blend in perfectly against the background reef. Scorpionfish wait absolutely motionless until an unsuspecting fish swims close enough to lunge.

The most common predators on the reef, the groupers, are also well camouflaged. They belong to a large family of fish that encompasses the little basslets and the enormous jewfish, which can reach over 2 metres (6.6 feet) in length and weigh as much as 700 kilograms (1540 pounds). Groupers are smaller but heavy-bodied, with large heads and very big mouths full of small, very sharp, backward-pointing teeth. They come in all sorts of colours and designs including red with dark spots, cream with red spots, and banded with purple spots. Most groupers are capable of changing colour to match their background. They change colour as they mature from a juvenile to an adult, when moving location, and may do so in a flash when startled. Like the scorpionfish, a grouper will often lurk, hidden on the reef, waiting for a small fish to swim by. When it is close enough, all the grouper has to do is open its huge mouth and the prey is literally sucked in. Another hunting strategy used by some is to swim very, very slowly along the reef. The prey, lulled into a false sense of security, allows the grouper to ease its way closer until it is within lunging distance.

The Nassau grouper is a very common sight on Caribbean reefs. Although not as large as the giant groupers of Cod Hole, only growing to about 1.3 metres (4.3 feet) in length, this fish is equally captivating. We found a particularly friendly male grouper in the Caymans. As soon as we entered the water he started making his way over to us, and by the time we had reached the sandy bottom, he was only a metre or so away. Slowly we befriended this large fish and he eventually let us stroke him and tickle his chin. The Nassau grouper has eight colour phases, varying from a light creamy beige to very dark brown, with bands that can change in prominence independently. This male had irregular, broad brown bars running down his body which blended well with the reef near us. Then he crossed the sand and his colour changed to a lighter tone with the bars still visible but much fainter.

As the afternoon wears on, the low angle of the light sharpens silhouettes and renders fish easy prey for hunters from below. It is then that predators begin to hunt more actively and there is a corresponding change in the behaviour of their potential prey. Midwater fish make their way down to the relative safety of the reef. Movement about the reef is no longer a leisurely search for food, but instead a purposeful quest. Solitary fish cluster together before migrating to find their habitual sleeping places, often deeper on the reef. Fish seem tense and are easily spooked as predators appear in the encroaching gloom.

Among the predators active at dusk are the jacks. They are strong, swift silvery fish that tend to live in open water bordering the reef. Typically they are seen emerging out of the blue haze beyond the drop-off, swimming with graceful ease in small groups. When they are hunting, their prey is probably totally unaware of the impending disaster, for they attack with lightning speed in a flash of silver, scattering all the fish on the reef.

Another group of predators that use speed, the barracuda, are greatly feared by humans as well as by their prey. Of the three species found in the Caribbean, the great barracuda is by far the biggest. Barracuda are voracious killers, rarely exceeding 2 metres (6.6 feet) in length, with long, jutting lower jaws and an alarming array of fang-like teeth. With their silver, torpedo-shaped bodies they can swim very fast.

OVERLEAF, LEFT: Blue chromis speckle the water above the reef in their search for plankton.
RIGHT: The territorial four-eye butterflyfish will raise its dorsal fin when threatened.

Confirmed reports of barracuda attacking people are few and far between, and such attacks have usually occurred in murky water where visibility is limited. Since barracuda rely on sight rather than smell to locate their prey, these attacks are probably mistakes. But this is of little comfort to a diver being followed by one. It is always unnerving to glimpse out of the corner of one's eye a large barracuda cruising by, despite knowing that it will almost certainly not attack. Their prey are less fortunate, for barracuda streak through a school of fish, often plankton eaters who are vulnerable in midwater, snapping up their victims before they have a chance to escape.

More intimidating even than the barracuda are the sharks. One of the most elegant is the silky shark, and we moved to the Bahamas in order to swim with them out in blue water. Like all sharks, they have denticles in their skin, but those of the silky shark are smaller and flatter than those of any other shark, making their skin fabulously silky to the touch. They are coloured a shimmering grey-brown on their back fading to white underneath, such countershading being found in many open water animals.

Silky sharks are the tropical equivalent of the blue sharks of temperate seas, and nearly as common. As with the blue sharks, we used bait to draw them in, but this time we dived without the protection of shark suits or a cage to retreat into. We were over the Tongue of the Ocean, with a 2000 metre (6600 foot) drop beneath us and no point of reference other than the boat's hull. It was hard work swimming against the current to maintain position in the water, instead of holding on to a cage.

There was nothing around us but blue with perhaps a hint of something moving in the haze. Then the silky sharks swam in from the seemingly empty sea and soon surrounded us. We kept our fingers well tucked in for, to a shark, fingers look temptingly bite sized. When a silky shark becomes aggressive it adopts a hunch-backed threat posture but this warning signal would have done us little good at such close range. As usual, though, a very rational sense of danger was replaced by awe at the creatures around us. The silky sharks were particularly wonderful to watch because they swam sinuously with grace and ease, in a manner quite unlike the twitchy grey reef sharks in Australia. We patted the sharks, stroked their flanks and gripped their tails, rather as one would a puppy.

We were also able to stroke their stomachs, having been taught a trick that allowed us to turn the shark over on to its back and cradle it for about ten seconds while it remained in a trance. One person held the tail and dorsal fin giving the other a chance to feel its underside which really was as smooth as silk. The only hitch was that when the shark 'woke up' it would swim off very fast and we had to avoid being in its path at this time.

Periodically we would make a concerted effort to get nearer to the boat, and the sharks always followed us. They would pick up the scent of the fish in our pockets and approach fast from downstream, swerving their way towards us. With slow powerful strokes of their bodies, they would glide up to us and hang back near our flipppers. It felt very strange swimming along on my back with 2 metre (6.6 foot) long sharks cruising at my feet.

Like the blue sharks, silky sharks live in open water as adults and feed on various fish and squid. They have excellent hearing and are sensitive to frequencies lower than those humans can hear, allowing them to detect the movements of schools of fish and squid at great distances. Slim with long pectoral fins, they are good long-distance swimmers and can attain high speeds in the chase. They are usually found at depths of 100 to 300 metres (330–1000 feet), but do hunt in shallower water and also migrate there to give birth to live young.

Male silky sharks mature after six years when they are over 2 metres (6.6 feet) long, and the females after seven or more years when they are a little bigger. The males and females can reach 2.8 metres (9.2 feet) and 3.3 metres (10.8 feet) respectively. Like many sharks they are segregated by sex, probably to reduce predation on each other, and only come together to breed. The females have a two-year breeding cycle. They carry their young for 12 months and give birth in late spring. They then mate and store the sperm until the following spring when they ovulate and their eggs are fertilised. This gives them a recovery time of approximately a year, without wasting the opportunity to mate. The pups are some 75 centimetres (30 inches) long at birth, and live for a while in shallow water near reefs or estuaries. They gradually move out and are living in deeper water by their first winter.

Following dusk on the reef, there is a period of quiet. The fish active in the daytime have assumed their drab night-time coloration and retreated to the relative safety of favourite sleeping sites. These sites may have been recently vacated by nocturnal fish, such as the grunts. They rest by day in big schools on the reef, and at nightfall make their precarious way past predators lying in wait to feed on nearby seagrass beds. They have a dull coloration and their camouflage is further enhanced by a mottling of their skin. At daybreak they return, transporting quantities of nutrients from the seagrass beds to the reef. This source of food significantly increases the growth rates of corals.

The night-time reef is the realm of the invertebrates. Many of these are extremely

ABOVE: The exquisite queen angelfish.
BELOW: Barracuda – an intimidating fish.

RIGHT: The Nassau grouper we befriended in the Caymans.

vulnerable and would suffer heavy losses if they emerged during the day. So it is only under the cover of dark that they creep out of nooks and crannies in the reef to forage for themselves. Featherstars, or crinoids, find an elevated spot on the reef from which to strain out food from the current. They hold their arms high and catch passing plankton using small branches called pinnules projecting from each arm. Featherstars only have a loose grasp on the rock, and must retreat to cover when the sea is rough.

Brittlestars squirm their way out of sponges and other unlikely corners of the reef using their snake-like arms. They also strain the water for plankton by holding their arms up into the current. The particles of food are trapped by the sticky mucus that lines the underside of the arms, and are passed down by hundreds of tube feet (tiny replicas of those on the crown of thorns starfish) to the mouth in the middle of the penny-sized central disc. Brittlestars would be extremely vulnerable feeding in the light of day, and even at night they may be taken by scavenging crabs. If trapped by an arm, they will simply break it off, the ease with which they can do this having given rise to their name. The animal rapidly moves out of danger, and within a few weeks the arm will have regrown.

Some species of brittlestar have another defence; they emit light or luminesce when touched, and even the slightest contact with something floating by will produce a little glow. The yellow-green flashes of light these species emit tend to deter predators. It was thought that the flashes might startle or blind the predator for an instant, giving the brittlestar time to escape. It now seems that, like brilliant coloration, the flashes signal danger, for the species that luminesce contain chemicals that make them unpalatable to predators. By warning the predator of its distastefulness, the brittlestar increases its chances of escaping unharmed. Wherever there is protection, some creatures will always exploit it, and small hermit crabs and shrimps can often be found sheltering in the arms of luminescent brittlestars.

Other nocturnal creatures of the reef, the sea urchins, belong to the same group as brittlestars and starfish. All these echinoderms or 'spiny skinned' animals are radially symmetrical, and have tube feet and powers of regeneration, although sea urchins mend rather than totally replace damaged parts. Sea urchins crawl out of crevices at night using their spines and tube feet, and graze on algae. They are voracious grazers and create 'halos' around small reefs by eating the seagrass within reach of their refuges. Each has a home range and forages within it in a surprisingly efficient way, generally not grazing the same area of reef on successive nights.

Sea urchins also have shelter sites to which they return after feeding and, in areas where predators abound, such sites are vital and are sought faithfully at dawn. They are far from defenceless, though, as the long-spined sea urchin exemplifies. This animal is justly named, for while its body only attains 10 centimetres (4 inches) in diameter, its hollow, needle-like spines can be 30 centimetres (12 inches) long. The spines are so sharp they easily penetrate wetsuits and human skin. They are also brittle, break easily, have minute backward-pointing barbs that make them extremely difficult to remove and they hurt a great deal. The effectiveness of this defence is enhanced by light sensitive cells all over the urchin's body. These cells detect any shadow falling on the urchin, and it swiftly orients the spines towards the potential attacker.

Sea urchins are plentiful on the reefs at night, but this was not so a few years ago. In the early 1980s, long-spined sea urchins were hit by the most widespread of any epidemic affecting marine invertebrates to date. The epidemic was first observed in Panama in January 1983, and only one year later the entire Caribbean was affected. The disease was probably a water-borne one, for the pattern of its spread followed the paths of surface currents. In the mass mortality that resulted, Caribbean populations of long-spined sea urchins were reduced to less than 1 per cent of their original numbers.

The lack of these urchins had profound effects on other reef life. Without the urchins' continual grazing, there was an immediate increase in algal growth, followed by an increase in the numbers of herbivorous fish, such as parrotfish and surgeonfish. The prolific algae competed with encrusting corals for space on the reef, but only seriously affected one species of hard coral. The queen triggerfish, which feeds mainly on sea urchins, reacted by switching to crustaceans, particularly crabs, and molluscs. Fortunately, the urchin population recovered swiftly and now the reefs, seagrass beds and mangroves all have their complement of long-spined sea urchins.

Coral polyps can also emerge more safely at night while the butterflyfish are nestled in a comatose state in the reef. Corals feed on the night bounty of the tiny animals that spend the day in deeper water. These zooplankton migrate towards the surface at night to feed on the tiny plants or phytoplankton living in the water column. The corals cannot follow their prey into midwater, but some fish do and stray quite far from the reef in search of food.

The cardinalfish hang motionless throughout the day, well hidden in caves, and venture forth cautiously at dusk to feed on the rising zooplankton. They are small fish, only about 10 centimetres (4 inches) in length, with large eyes that can gather a lot of light and so allow good night vision. They also have large mouths, and the male uses his during the breeding season to incubate the eggs he has fertilised.

Brittlestar emerges from a sponge; its daytime refuge.

Cardinalfish are mostly red, a colour that provides camouflage at night because the blue water absorbs red wavelengths of light, making anything red appear as either grey or black.

Like cardinalfish and many other nocturnal fish, blackbar soldierfish are red, have big eyes and secrete themselves in caves during the day. They generally forage alone, feeding on the abundant zooplankton and other creatures. They are larger than cardinalfish, reaching 20 centimetres (8 inches) in length, and their close relatives, the squirrelfish, are larger still, about 30 centimetres (12 inches) long. Squirrelfish are thinner and more aquiline than their cousins, and are more difficult for predators to handle, being covered in very sharp scales and spines. Again they forage alone, but on the reef rather than in midwater, commonly taking crabs and shrimps.

There are also much larger predators hunting on the reef at night including moray eels which feed on sleeping fish, crabs and molluscs. Morays have a reputation for being vicious, aggressive and dangerous. In reality, although they will retaliate if provoked, they are timid creatures and shelter in holes during the day, with their bodies well anchored in the rock. It is rare, but possible, to see them fully exposed in daylight, and rarer still to see them free swimming in the darkness of night.

I had the opportunity to encounter a green moray eel during the daytime, a chance I could not turn down. Feeling more curious than confident, I dived down to its refuge. The very large, 1.5 metre (5 foot) long eel had no hesitation in coming out of its cave at the smell of the fish I had with me. It was equally prepared to approach me and let me handle it. Moray eels are wonderfully smooth to the touch, because they have no scales. This particular eel's flesh seemed to give way in my grasp as it slithered through my hands, winding its way around me in its quest for food. I happily held him, stroked him, fed him and finally watched him retreat back into his home.

Morays have large mouths with an irregular array of slender, sharp, spike-like teeth. They need a continuous flow of water through their mouths and over their gills to breathe, and so are typically seen opening and closing their mouths, a habit that makes them look more intimidating than they actually are. Some have a dragon-like appearance due to two tubular nostrils that stick well out from the head. Even the morays without such nostrils have a keen sense of smell, for this is how they detect their prey.

Dolphins, on the other hand, can draw on a number of highly developed senses when seeking their prey. Dolphins (and whales) were land creatures during one stage of their long evolutionary history, and on returning to water their predecessors found an environment already dominated by other large predators, the sharks. In order to survive, they had to swim fast enough to catch prey and still surface to breathe. They also had to develop ways of detecting prey and predators in murky or deep water where vision is of limited use. They have adapted to cope with these and other challenges remarkably well.

Dolphins are spindle-shaped, streamlined mammals which swim with an undulating motion, only possible because of their very flexible backbone. The most obvious difference in swimming technique between dolphins and fish is that dolphins propel themselves by moving their tail up and down rather than from side to side. In this way they can reach speeds of over 40 km/h (25 mph). Their skin and underlying muscles are specially modified to reduce vibration and turbulence at high speeds and so reduce drag. Even so, how they achieve the speeds they do is not fully understood, for theoretical calculations predict a significantly slower rate of motion.

Many people have had the thrill of seeing dolphins enjoying a free ride in the bow wave of a boat. Fewer have been fortunate enough to swim with wild dolphins at sea. In the Bahamas we went in search of them, and to our delight found a group of 50–100 spotted dolphins. Adult spotted dolphins have grey backs and near white undersides covered, as their name suggests, with hundreds of contrasting spots, white along the back and dark underneath. Each subadult and adult dolphin has a unique set of markings, allowing an individual to be identified easily. There are also discernible patterns that are shared by groups within a region but vary between groups from different regions. The juveniles have no spots and become increasingly mottled as they mature.

The group we came across live on the Little Bahama Bank and so they do not have to range far for food because ample prey is to be found in deeper water just off the shallow sand flats. The banks offer an alternative source of food and protection from predators, such as the tiger sharks and pilot whales, that roam in deeper water. The dolphins' home waters are very clear and shallow and, in good weather, almost like a swimming pool.

Diving with the dolphins required dogged determination, for they have a very short attention span. They frequently swam past the boat before we had a chance to get ready. So we put snorkellers in the water to keep the dolphins entertained until we had kitted up. But when we joined them, encumbered with scuba tanks and bubble helmets, we were unable to maintain their interest. After many false starts, we gave up the diving apparatus altogether and opted for the greater manoeuvrability of snorkelling gear.

LEFT, ABOVE: The moray eel's gaping jaw belies a timid nature. LEFT, BELOW: The large eyes of soldierfish aid nocturnal vision.

RIGHT: Tubastrea coral; (*above*) polyps withdrawn during the day, (*below*) polyps extended to feed at night.

Our more successful encounters were in rough weather, which increased our problems but made the dolphins more playful, surfing and jumping in the waves. On one occasion we went in off the back of the boat while the surge splashed violently through the dive platform. With broad grins we swam to meet the dolphins. The next hour was one of the most exhausting and exhilarating of my life. All my senses were alert and my body was pushed to its limits, lungs straining and heart pounding, as we dived, spun, twisted, surfaced for air and dived again, never letting up our antics for fear of losing the dolphins' attention.

Sometimes our roles were reversed and they would entice us to play. One dolphin picked up a piece of seaweed in her mouth, let it fall and caught it with her pectoral fin. She then brought it over to me, and turned and flapped her tail fluke, clearly indicating that I was invited to join in. She would not take the seaweed out of my hand, but would instantly swim over when I let it drop. Again, she collected it with her fins, pectoral or dorsal, rather than her mouth.

In between bouts of play, the dolphins sometimes foraged over the sand. They would swim slowly along the bottom, their beaks directed down and forward, and suddenly grab an unfortunate flounder that had risen from hiding. Like most animals they are opportunists and will take such easy prey at any time, but spotted dolphins feed mainly in the low light of dawn and dusk. They tackle schools of fish, often hunting cooperatively, and will pursue squid in deeper water. Where light is poor, they rely more heavily on echolocation, emitting regularly spaced clicks to find their prey.

At other times they rest and sleep on the banks in the relative safety of shallow water. Dolphins sleep by lolling or slowly moving at the surface with their blow hole exposed to the air. They are able to shut down one side of their brain and close one eye, while keeping the other open to maintain contact with the group and to watch for predators. For much of the day dolphins emit sounds but when sleeping and vulnerable, they avoid attracting attention to themselves by keeping relatively quiet.

Dolphins are very social animals, and spotted dolphins live in flexible groups, the compositions of which vary with age. Until they are 4 years old infant dolphins stay with their mothers, and from 4 to 8 years the juveniles spend their day in nursery groups, usually chaperoned by an older dolphin. They tend to separate into single sex groups from 9 to 14 years of age, the young adults taking it in turns to act as baby-sitter to the younger dolphins. These subgroups often forage on their own but will rejoin the adults to rest, when called. As adults they intermingle freely, large males being found with females and their infants.

Members of the group communicate with each other in a number of ways, including body posture and sound. Their ability to convey messages through body posturing is enhanced by the dolphins' all round vision, for they can even see beneath their beak and follow the movements of dolphins directly below. The significance of a particular posture or movement varies with the individual or context. For example, a slight turn can initiate a chase between two older dolphins, while a roll by an infant is a signal that it wants to suckle. The mother will respond by presenting her underside and, after the infant has stimulated the teat to protrude, the mother will squirt a very rich milk into its mouth. A fuller turn between two adults is sexual, particularly if the underside is presented below the partner.

Some signals utilise both posture and sound. Various combinations of these signals greatly increase the scope for communication. Tail slaps can call attention, such as those used by the baby-sitter to summon wayward juveniles, or they can indicate annoyance. Breaching may be purely playful, or its purpose may be to call attention or to remove parasites. Blowing bubbles often indicates aggression or annoyance and is commonly seen when two dolphins are fighting beak to beak. It is also used by a mother when something comes between her and her infant.

The young are given no formal training, and the postures, and how to hunt and behave, are learnt mainly through mimicry. The instinct to mimic is so strong that, when we were with them, the dolphins soon copied our movements. We dived down, hung vertically in the water and the dolphins did the same. We spun around in the water and they circled with us. Eye contact proved very important, and if we lost it for an instant our playmates would temporarily swim off. In order to gain their trust, we swam with our legs together and our hands by our sides, trying, as far as is possible, to look like dolphins. To change direction, we turned our heads very slightly, still watching them, and they followed. Often we would be surrounded by six or more dolphins, only inches away, and the precision of their swimming was never more clearly demonstrated than at such times. Their proximity was tantalising but we had to resist every urge to touch them, for they never initiated contact.

Within their groups, though, dolphins are very tactile animals. When a mother is reunited with her infant, she will touch it with her pectoral fins, and the infant responds by doing the same. She steers it by covering its dorsal fin with her tail fluke,

OVERLEAF, ABOVE LEFT: A spotted dolphin emits bubbles while producing a signature whistle.

BELOW LEFT: Contact is an important form of communication between dolphins. RIGHT: While conveying a message, the body posturing of dolphins is also sublimely graceful.

usually staying above it. A common form of contact throughout the group is pectoral fin rubbing, and dolphins will often swim along facing each other with pectoral fins touching. Adults will calm down excited youngsters by touching them, while mothers, siblings or baby-sitters will discipline young dolphins if and when they get out of hand by pushing them into the sand with their beaks.

Sexual contact between members of the group is also common. They will sexually stimulate each other from a very early age and continue to do so throughout their lives. They use their pectoral fins to stimulate the genital region of dolphins of the same or opposite sex and of different ages. This open sexuality serves to strengthen bonds within the group.

Sound plays a particularly important part in the dolphins' daily lives. As with body posture, young dolphins learn the acoustic signals they will need through mimicry. Echolocation clicks are used by dolphins to orientate themselves and to navigate, as well as to detect prey. They also emit clicks in bursts, which sound more like bleats or squawks. These sounds are used more in interaction within the group than the more evenly spaced clicks of echolocation, although the origin of the sound is the same. Sounds easily mimicked by dolphins may also be used to communicate with other dolphin species, for example, to exchange appeasement signals.

Whistles, which can travel long distances, are yet another form of audible communication. One type of whistle, the contact call, can be heard by dolphins over 3 kilometres (1.9 miles) away, and is used for regrouping, or between a mother and her infant. The most fascinating whistle of all is the signature whistle. Each dolphin has its own particular sound which is recognised by all the other dolphins in the group. If members of the group want to attract the attention of an individual, they will emit its particular signature whistle. Usually, but not always, bubbles come out of the blow hole when signature whistles are made. Interestingly, young males have signature whistles very like that of their mother, while young females do not. Years after leaving the family group and becoming sexually mature, the male will be able to identify his mother by her similar signature whistle and avoid mating with her.

In addition to the echolocation clicks, the squawks and the signature whistles, spotted dolphins make 30 other sounds. They can produce more than one type of sound simultaneously, and the looping and repetition of particular noises convey different meanings. All these sounds, combined with their body postures, give dolphins a sophisticated communication system which we have barely begun to understand.

As people increasingly explore the oceans we are gradually discovering the extent to which marine animals communicate. In order to feed and reproduce successfully, and to avoid being eaten, most groups of animals have evolved some form of signalling between individuals. Many of the reef fish convey information using colour and body language, while invertebrates may use these methods as well as chemical cues. Again, the meanings of most of these signals are as yet far beyond our comprehension. Trying to understand the motivation and effects of communications in the underwater world is a fascinating challenge, and one to which man is beginning to rise. Of all the noises heard in the oceans perhaps the most intriguing are the haunting sounds emitted by one of the animals at our next location, the humpback whales of Hawaii.

THE HAWAIIAN ISLANDS

Midway across the North Pacific, space, time, and life uniquely interlace a chain of islands named 'Hawaiian'. Charles Lindbergh.

Set amid the vast emptiness of the Pacific Ocean, the Hawaiian Islands come as a welcome relief to the eye. From the deep blue waters rise towering mountains, their upper slopes blanketed by trees and dripping with mosses and ferns. The easily eroded black, sometimes ochre, lava and ash from older volcanoes, long since dormant, have worn away over many thousands of years to yield steep, razor sharp ridges, precipitous gullies and sheer pinnacles. Hundreds of waterfalls carve the land into ravines, and join forces to create rivers that scour away the rock, forming ever deepening canyons. One, now over 600 metres (2000 feet) deep, is called the Grand Canyon of the Pacific.

Hawaii is one of the few places on this planet where arctic conditions exist amongst the warm wetness of the subtropics, for the archipelago incorporates the tallest mountains in the world. The volcano Mauna Kea rises some 10 200 metres (33 476 feet) from the deep ocean, although only 4200 metres (13 796 feet) protude above the surface. Hawaii's younger volcanoes, some only 750 000

A patina of vegetation does little to disguise the layers of lava of which the Hawaiian islands are made.

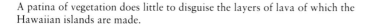

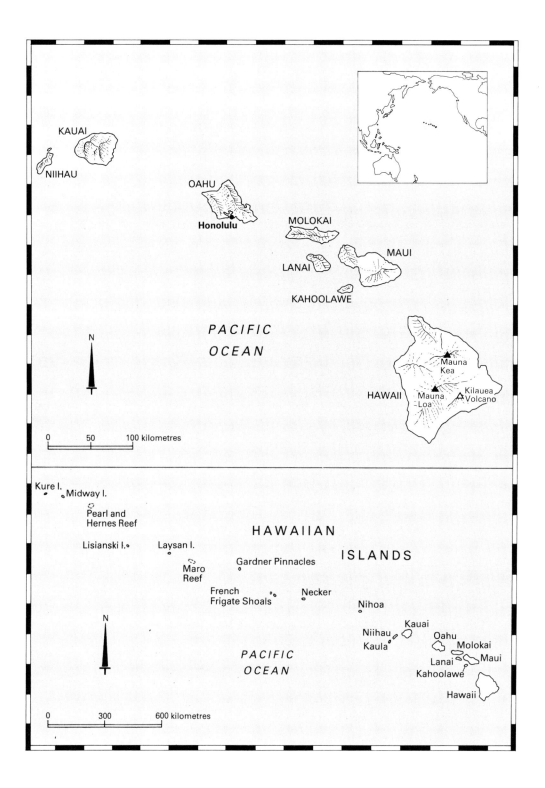

years old, are snow capped. Lava fields carpet the lower slopes of these active volcanoes and are added to year by year, destroying much in the process. In time, the activity dies down and erosion wears away the mountains, easing the way for colonists. The now extinct volcanoes of the older islands are lower and provide a safe home for a stable community of plants and animals.

Hawaii's extreme isolation in the Pacific has limited the number of creatures that it harbours. Among the very few animals found in Hawaii that can cross such vast expanses of ocean regularly and with ease are the humpback whales. Having spent the summer feeding in the temperate or near-polar waters of the northern Pacific, they travel some 10 000 kilometres (6200 miles) to the warmer waters of Hawaii for the winter. Humpbacks all over the world migrate to breed in tropical waters. Those of the north-west Atlantic go to winter in the Caribbean and, six months later, a group from the Antarctic find the Great Barrier Reef a safe haven to bear their young. With one exception, a population of humpbacks in the Indian Ocean, those living in the northern hemisphere probably do not mix with southern populations, a separation similar to that of sperm whales. This low level of intermixing is sustained by the way in which individuals learn the migration route. Calves follow their mothers during their first year, and thereafter keep to the same trail. Within each hemisphere, though, populations do intermingle. Some of the humpbacks that spend the winter in Hawaii share their summer waters in Alaska with whales that have come up from Mexico.

We found the humpbacks easy to identify. They have flat, large heads that comprise a third of the total body length of 12–15 metres (40–50 feet). The dark, almost black, body sports some white on the flippers, tail and underside, the extent of which varies between individuals. A small, curved dorsal fin sits on the platform of blubber from which the humpback gets its name. When these whales dive they rise out of the water and bend their backs, exaggerating the lump or hump. They sometimes raise their tails right out of the water as they dive, revealing the white patterning and distinctive serration of the flukes by which individual whales can be recognised.

Their Latin name, *Megaptera*, translates as 'great wing' and refers to their exceptionally long flippers. These modified forelimbs are typically a third of their body length, and are the longest flippers of any whale. The leading edge of each flipper is deformed by small lumps, or tubercles, on which one species of barnacle grows, while

OVERLEAF: Blowing a warning stream of bubbles, a male humpback whale defends his position as 'escort' to a female and her calf. The retreating challenger is just visible in the background.

the tubercles on their lips and the tips of the tail flukes are colonised by another. During their time in cold water, humpbacks can accumulate a load of up to 450 kilograms (990 pounds) of barnacles. One of the advantages of breeding in warm water is that the barnacles often die and fall off. The relief is short-lived, however, for they are soon replaced by whale lice, which are tiny crustaceans resembling ticks.

Being a cosmopolitan species, humpbacks were persecuted by the whalers of the nineteenth and early twentieth centuries throughout the world's oceans. Their slow cruising speed of between 2 and 5 km/h (1–3 mph), their curiosity, and their habits of feeding mainly inshore and breeding in shallow tropical waters at a predictable location, all rendered them easy targets. Even small coastal operations could tackle these whales with hand harpoons. In addition, their high concentration of oil meant that the dead whales did not sink and were easily floated to shore. Of a population in excess of 100 000 in the southern hemisphere at the beginning of this century, more than 60 000 were slaughtered just between 1910 and 1916. By 1963 numbers had been reduced to a total of less than 5000 and, humpback whaling in the region having become economically unviable, a ban was at last enforced. Protection came as recently as 1966 for all other humpback populations.

Today, only a few indigenous peoples are allowed to hunt a limited number of humpbacks, and they can only use traditional methods. The whales still face threats, though, such as competition with fishermen for the ever decreasing fish stocks. Humpbacks are not frightened of boats or of fishing gear and often get caught in nets, in particular those of the cod fishermen off Newfoundland. Although teams dedicated to their rescue regularly free these entangled giants, not all survive. In Hawaii, as elsewhere, by far the most serious threat is loss of habitat. Female whales nursing newly born calves seek the calm protected waters in the lee of the islands, and these are ideal for para-sailing and jet skiing. For the time being, such activities have been banned during the humpback's breeding season. Run-off from agricultural land and other pollution is also beginning to limit the breeding and feeding grounds available to the whales. Despite these pressures, protection is beginning to show significant effects and, worldwide, the population is thought to be over twice as large as it was when whaling was stopped. But it will be many decades before the humpback begins to approach its former abundance.

Described by Herman Melville as 'the most gamesome and light-hearted ... making more gay foam and white water than any other', humpbacks do seem to be the most exuberant of whales. Rolling, lunging, slapping the water, splashing and breaching, whereby they rise high out of the water and fall back with a mighty crash, are all part of their repertoire. In the animal world such energetic pursuits usually have a function, and those of the humpbacks are probably a means of communication. Signalling becomes important for the males on their arrival in Hawaii because they need to win access to females in the face of considerable competition from their peers.

Humpbacks seem to breach more in strong winds, possibly because of the need to create a louder signal or maybe just for pure enjoyment. While we were there, breaching was particularly common on the exposed part of the coast where a 75 km/h (40 knot) wind was blowing. One whale breaching will trigger others to rise up as we saw on our first day with the humpbacks, when we were following a particularly active group of eight or so whales. One breached high in the air, falling back with a tremendous splash, and four others followed suit in quick succession, making the water white with foam.

On another occasion, we had the great good fortune to witness the start of a breach from underwater. A male suddenly appeared close to us, powering itself vertically upwards with huge strokes of its tail. As it surfaced, we lifted our heads out of the water and saw it rise up only 8 metres (26 feet) away. In true breaching, which happens 80 per cent of the time, the whale turns in mid-breach and crashes down on its back. The less stylised breach, in which it does not turn, resembles a gigantic belly flop. Each individual may perform a series of breaches, and one calf was seen to breach over 250 times in a row. Another calf breached completely out of the water near our boat. It is rare but not unknown for adult humpbacks to leave the water totally when breaching. The effort of lifting up a body weighing some 36 tonnes must be considerable and successive breaches may become weaker with less of the whale being seen.

Lunging is an altogether less dramatic manœuvre, bringing only up to 40 per cent of the body out of the water. Again, it occurs mainly amongst males competing to acquire a female. The repeated breaching and lunging presumably allow other whales, both male and female, to assess an individual's strength and stamina. The fantastic noise created by breaching carries a great deal further than any visual signal, such as body posturing, and so many more whales will receive the message. Slapping the water with a flipper creates a noise like a rifle shot but the sound does not travel as far. The sound that travels furthest of all, some 9–10 kilometres (6 miles), is the most distinctive and famous of all whale noises – the song of the humpback.

Only male humpbacks sing, and they do so predominantly during the breeding season. Parts of the song are heard during their summer feeding and the occurrence of singing increases as they migrate to their breeding grounds. The eerie, plaintive

LEFT: Blithely unaware of her human audience, a female humpback whale tail slaps to attract distant suitors.
RIGHT: The most exuberant of whales, humpbacks are noted for frequent breaching. Function or fun, they breach both here off Hawaii and while in their Alaskan feeding grounds.

sounds are easily heard through the hull of a boat and have led many a sailor to think his ship haunted. Often when I was snorkelling below the surface chop, the ocean seemed to be filled with the whales' song. The singing is composed of moans, groans, roars, chirps, cries and squeals. The separate noises form phrases which are grouped into themes and these are strung together to form the song. The humpbacks' song is the longest and most varied in the animal world, lasting between 6 and 30 minutes before being repeated.

Unlike sperm whales and spotted dolphins, individual humpbacks do not have their own signature sounds and instead share a song within the group. Thus the humpbacks in Hawaii have a different song from that of another population, just as killer whales have local dialects. The song of a group of humpbacks is not permanently fixed but changes through the breeding season, all the males learning and incorporating the variations. Like breaching, singing may be a method of sorting out a dominance order between males. During the song, there are jumps and gaps when the singer breathes. The longer the uninterrupted song, the bigger the lungs and, probably, the size of the singer. This extraordinary breath-holding contest is a very effective sexual display, and when one male starts singing, others in the vicinity respond by variously retreating, attacking or adopting a submissive role.

As competition between sexually active males increases, so does the aggression, and tail slapping, lunging, rolling and head butting become more common. A male 'escorting' a female and her calf will not be singing and is often challenged by other males. The female may even entice other males to her by repeatedly slapping her flippers on the surface. We frequently saw groups ploughing through the water with a female and her calf in the lead, the escort near her side and challengers following. On one occasion a fight broke out in front of us, the challengers trying to displace the escort by lunging, charging, tail swiping and striking at him. His head bloodied and his dorsal fin broken, the escort persevered during the 2 hours we stayed with the group. Such battles can continue for days.

I received a close-up view of a male in fighting mode when we were underwater, ahead of a group. The mother and her calf swam peacefully past, but the escort started blowing bubbles from his mouth, a sure sign of aggression. Suddenly he turned and headed directly towards me and, terrified, I swam backwards as fast as I could. Then, to my great relief, I saw the escort ram a challenger that had come up alongside me. At the height of his rise, the escort was right in front of me and the force from a flick of his tail pushed me back in the water. As I recovered the whales disappeared behind a curtain of bubbles.

Eventually the losers move off leaving the mother and calf in peace. The victor becomes the escort and hopes to have the chance to mate with the female. Courtship, when it commences, is an altogether less violent affair. The male lies on his back at the surface, slapping the water with alternate flippers. He may also raise himself horizontally in the water and sink down again, and will roll towards the female. They will touch and pat each other with their flippers and rub heads. Nothing is known about the eventual act of mating in humpbacks, for it has never been observed.

The young develops in the mother for nearly a year, and so the calf is born en route to or in the same waters in which it was conceived. At birth it weighs about 1300 kilograms (2900 pounds) and is some 4 metres (13 feet) long. The mother may mate soon after giving birth, but will more usually wait a year. She stays close to her calf and is often accompanied by a male escort. We usually found such trios resting peacefully in shallower water. The first time we swam slowly over to get a closer look, the escort was hanging vertically in the water and the mother was just below him, also vertical, and sleeping. Unusually, the calf was resting against the escort's belly rather than its mother's. Calves have to breathe every few minutes and soon this one moved lazily up to the surface for air. Then it saw us and swam over to get a better look, and we realised that the 'little' calf was about 5 metres (15 feet) long. Alarmed at our proximity, it swiped its tail and went back down to the escort, which was now horizontal in the water with flippers splayed outwards. Some minutes later the female came up to breathe and this 15 metre (45 foot) whale turned towards me, gave me a long, steady gaze and swam by, its pectoral fins missing my face by inches. With the calf on top, the trio eventually swam off in an unhurried way, undulating their backs for propulsion.

Mothers and their calves are the last to leave the warm waters of Hawaii for the long migration to Alaska, during which the mother may start to feed again. The calf suckles for up to a year and grows fast during this time, for it takes large amounts of milk each day. This places a considerable demand on the mother, especially if she is pregnant with her next calf, and while in northern waters she must rebuild her reserves.

Humpbacks are social all year, and in the rich feeding grounds of Alaska they even cooperate in hunting. Instead of teeth, the humpback's mouth houses between 270 and 400 baleen plates, each 65 centimetres (25 inches) or so long and covered in

OVERLEAF, LEFT: The eroding forces of rain and seawater have shaped the Hawaiian islands.
RIGHT: Remnants of a lava tube form cathedral-like arches underwater.

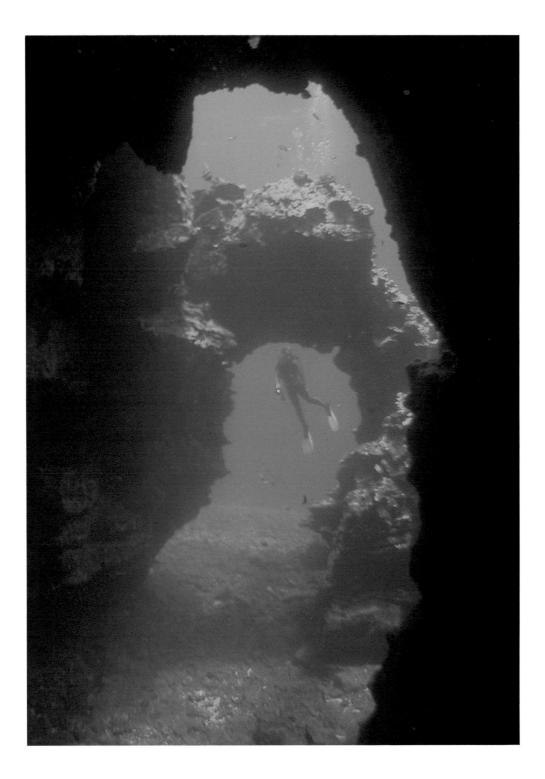

coarse bristles. Twenty or so impressive ventral grooves run back from the chin, some extending as far as the navel, and these allow a fantastic expansion of the mouth and throat during feeding. Their diet consists mainly of krill and shoaling fish such as herring, sand eels, capelin and mackerel, which tend to live densely, if patchily, within 50 metres (160 feet) of the surface.

Humpbacks lunge to capture prey at the surface, both food and water spilling out as they close their gaping mouths. They may concentrate prey before scooping them up, using their tails to form rings of foam, or using bubbles issuing from the mouth or blow hole. The bubbles may either erupt in a single cloud that confuses the prey or form a curtain next to the prey as the whale swims along. The most impressive technique of all is bubble netting, which may be done singly or in a group. The humpbacks start by making a synchronised ascent from a depth of 15 metres (50 feet) or so, well below their intended prey. They release air from their blow holes to create a circle of bubbles that traps the prey. The whales then rise up within the circle with their mouths open and engulf gallons of water along with the food. At the height of their tremendous splashing rise from the water, they close their mouths and their huge ventral grooves expand to accommodate the bulk. Their tongues force water out through the mouth and the hairy baleen plates sieve the nutritious food which is then swallowed. After a summer of intensive feeding the humpbacks have regained their lost weight and strength, and are ready to start their journey back to Hawaii.

It is little wonder that few other animals can travel there regularly. Sited in the middle of the Pacific, well over 3000 kilometres (1900 miles) from the nearest continent and 1600 kilometres (1000 miles) from any other island, Hawaii is the most remote island group in the world. The Hawaiian chain has been formed in much the same way as the Galápagos Islands, by molten lava breaking through the Earth's crust at a weak place or hot spot.

The Hawaiian Islands rest on the Pacific plate which once moved in a northerly direction. So the submarine mountains known as the Emperor Seamounts, which were created over the hot spot about 70 million years ago, are scattered in a north–south direction. These now lie eroded beneath the waves to the north-west of the Hawaiian Islands. About 43 million years ago the plate began moving at a rate of 6 centimetres (2.5 inches) a year in a north-westerly direction and, as a result, the more recent Hawaiian chain of mountains lies along that axis on the Hawaiian Ridge. This stretches from Kure, which is the oldest, most westerly island and now merely an atoll, to the youngest, most easterly mountain, which has not yet risen above the water's surface but has already been given the name Loihi. Within this enormous archipelago there are hundreds of atolls, pinnacles and islands, of which only eight are of appreciable size. These extend over 650 kilometres (400 miles) of ocean from Niihau, just west of Kauai, the oldest at over 5 million years, to Hawaii or the Big Island, which is the youngest, having emerged less than a million years ago.

Pele, the islanders' legendary goddess of fire, now lives on Big Island beneath the volcano of Kilauea. She is an untameable spirit, famous for the rivers and curtains of orange lava that issue forth from the active crater. Hawaiian lava, known locally as *pahoehoe*, is a very fluid liquid that runs like water. When molten lava lakes burst their banks, it pours out and gushes in thick streams down the mountainside. The outer layer cools and hardens into a metallic grey crust, insulating the inner lava, which continues running as underground rivers at 1200°C (2200°F). The casing can be thin and may break in some places to reveal the hidden rush of molten rock. As the eruption quietens and the flow of lava slows, the rivers run dry creating tunnels known as lava tubes. Beneath the ground there is a network of such tubes, some cavernous and others too small to enter. Those on land were used by ancient Hawaiians as burial sites for their dead. Those underwater provide refuge for few marine animals but, as we discovered, they are spectacular sites to explore.

The underwater lava tube we entered was a series of arches, caverns and passageways that opened up into a large cathedral-like chamber. Within the giant grotto, shafts of sunlight filtered through gaps in the roof, relieving the gloom of the chamber and catching the bubbles rising from our helmets. There was little marine life apparent in this network of tunnels, besides the menacing whitetip reef sharks circling in and out of vision, and soldierfish, familiar to us from our encounters with their Caribbean cousins. These big-eyed, red fish hung secreted in the shadows where they spend their day before going out on to the reef to feed at night.

Pele is destructive on land, where she swamps and burns trees and homes, and, less frequently, underwater, where she destroys any corals that have managed to make a start in the vicinity. Fortunately for the developing corals, the lava only reaches the sea when Pele is particularly ferocious. Then the hot, molten lava meets the cold, quenching sea, and the gases in it explode like small bombs, blanketing the surface with steam and bubbles. The water quickly wins this battle and cools the lava from orange to black. As more lava flows, it continually breaks through fine cracks in the thin crust, giving it the appearance of an expanding underwater rock. Gradually, the drama subsides and the sea washes over the new layer of jagged black rock, eroding it day after day, year after year, into the black sands that characterise many of Hawaii's beaches. Thus Pele's work is deceptive, for while with one hand

LEFT: 'Skylights' are formed by a collapse in the roof of a lava tube, allowing a rare sight of flowing molten rock below.
RIGHT: Bursting through its crust, lava pours into quenching water.

she destroys, with the other she builds layer upon layer of rock, creating new land and underwater surfaces ripe for colonisation.

As in the Galápagos Islands, time and chance determined which species reached the Hawaiian islands and thereafter successfully colonised them. Tiny insects and spiders, and small spores, such as those of ferns, probably arrived on the high, icy cold, 300 kilometre per hour (190 mph) winds of the jet stream. The cold and the length of the journey have precluded this mode of transportation for most minute creatures. Seeds would have found the feathers, feet and digestive tracts of birds a surer way of reaching a new destination, for birds will seek land and preen themselves on arrival. It is thought that around 75 per cent of Hawaiian plants, a considerably higher percentage than in the Galápagos, were brought across the ocean by birds. While the Galápagos received rafts of vegetation from the nearby American mainland, the chances of such rafts drifting across the vastness of the Pacific and hitting Hawaii are minute. Seeds floating off distant atolls do manage the journey, though, and thousands of such seeds are washed up on Hawaii's beaches every year. They tend to remain beach plants, for they are not suited to colonising the steep wet hillsides.

These haphazard landfalls, both air- and water-borne, enabled eggs, seeds, larvae, spores, tiny insects and birds to begin the process of colonisation. At first sparse vegetation and then, in time, forests took hold and spread over the lava rock. The plants thrived in the rain brought by the north-east trade winds that blow across Hawaii. Forests now abound there and cloud-shrouded swamps lie hidden on the island of Kauai which is the wettest place on Earth, receiving an amazing 20 metres (790 inches) of rain each year. Swamps, wet forests, dry forests, lava deserts, steaming craters and snow-capped mountains are just some of the diverse habitats available to colonists. Without large mammals and reptiles to eat them, the birds, insects and snails also flourished. As new islands rose from the sea, these animals, along with many plants, colonised each in turn as if they were a row of stepping stones.

Also along these stepping stones came a species whose impact has been greater than any other's. Man, a comparatively recent colonist, has not had to change in order to exploit these islands. In contrast, as on the Galápagos, other creatures gradually adapted to their new home and the opportunities it offered. There are two main prerequisites for new species to evolve – a diversity of habitats and a significant distance from the source or original home. Hawaii provides both to a much greater degree than most other places, including the Galápagos. As a result it is regarded as the showplace of the process by which many different species evolve from a few ancestral types. For example, only about 250 species of plant are thought to have succeeded in colonising the islands, yet these have given rise to 1800 species. Without grazing mammals to eat them, the plant colonists no longer needed their original defences. Mint lost its smell, the holly lost its prickles and the now giant gooseberry lost its thorns. Insects have done even better, with an estimated 250 original species evolving into the impressive 4000 species now inhabiting the islands. Many of these have changed their habits, including a moth that does not fly and a caterpillar that eats meat. Among the birds are the Hawaiian equivalent of Darwin's famous finches, the honeycreepers. The 20 or so species found in the islands today are thought to be descended from one species of honeycreeper, and have since adapted to fill a great variety of niches, evolving different bills and plumages to suit their needs. Altogether, 15 species of land birds made it across the ocean, evolving into 80 species. Of these only 40 now remain, for as new habitats are created, by Pele and the action of rain and wind, some species adapt well, changing and establishing themselves, whilst others fall by the wayside. Extinctions have been rife in other groups as well, due to both natural causes and man's actions.

Before man introduced alien animals and plants, 99 per cent of Hawaii's land plants and 96 per cent of its land animals were found only in Hawaii. Underwater, a smaller proportion of species are endemic, with, for example, 30 per cent of the reef fish being found only there. Most of these species differ in comparatively minor ways from their relatives elsewhere in the Indo-Pacific. This shows that the sea is a relatively good vehicle for allowing the mixing of distant populations. Even so, Hawaii does have the highest proportion of endemic fish anywhere in the world.

While the extreme isolation of Hawaii's coral reefs has allowed unique species to evolve, it has also limited the number of colonisers and Hawaii has fewer species of fish than most other Indo-Pacific reefs. For example, Hawaii has a mere 420 species of inshore and reef fish, whereas the Philippines boast over 2000. Most of those living in Hawaii have arrived as larvae rather than adults, for larval fishes may drift and disperse great distances, and are well adapted to survive in the open ocean. The further they drift, though, the lower are their chances of successful colonisation. Hawaii must have been an extremely remote destination even for species like the moorish idol, which has large and very hardy larvae and so has been able to establish itself all round the tropical Indo-Pacific. It is thought that most of Hawaii's successful fish colonisers have, over time, come from the reefs of southern Japan because these two well-separated groups of islands have a surprisingly similar range of fish.

Some fish common on other reefs around the world simply have not managed

LEFT: Dragon eels are one of many species of moray eel that abound as predators on Hawaiian reefs.
RIGHT: Thanks to their large and robust larvae, moorish idols have been able to colonise reefs throughout the tropical Pacific.

the journey. The most notable absentees are the rabbitfish, fusiliers, snappers and groupers. Other creatures have filled their niches. For example, moray eels are particularly abundant on Hawaiian reefs, partly because they fill the groupers' role as reef predators and partly because, elsewhere, the groupers are among the juvenile morays' most frequent predators.

Hawaiians have many legends about the creation of their islands and the animals found there. In one such story, the god Kumuhonua gave each fish a role or duty to fulfil and in order to recognise them, he called them all together and marked them. Some he made yellow, some white, some he gave stripes, and others he merely sprinkled with ashes giving them a mottled appearance. One triggerfish is particularly beautiful in its adornment, with vivid red bars at the base of its blue pectoral fins, gold stripes and a gold-bordered black triangle near its tail. This is Hawaii's state fish and boasts the longest name of any fish in the world, humuhumu-nukunuku-a-pua'a, which in English means 'the fish which carries a needle and has a snout and grunts like a pig'.

Coral reef fish are famed for their bright, audacious coloration, often called flag or poster-coloration. While many of their colours are very visible to us from above, when seen side on in the water they tend to merge into the background. Blue is a relatively common colour among reef fish and, for example, the bluey-grey background colour of the ubiquitous sergeant major fish is lost against the blue haze of water. This leaves visible only its disconnected parallel dark bars, possibly rendering it unrecognisable as a fish to a would-be predator. In addition, many reef fish change colour as they move from one place to another, matching the background as they go. So at one time it was suggested that the colours of reef fish serve mainly to hide them against the water or the reef.

It is now generally thought that poster-coloration performs other functions besides camouflage. Bright colours are a form of self-advertisement and so may help to space competing fish over the reef. Many species of solitary damselfish have bright, often iridescent colours, whereas their more social counterparts are grey, brown, black or a dirty white. The naturalist Lorenz noted that only the most aggressive, territorial species, such as some of the damselfish, butterflyfish and surgeonfish, are brightly coloured. Any clash between members of such species is usually ritualised and serious aggression is seldom seen on the reef. This is probably due at least partly to colour signals, the very presence of a fish with startling colours in a certain place being advertisement enough of its dominance of that area. Where aggression does occur, it is usually between two individuals of the same size. This suggests that colour signals may be used by fish, like the songs and posturing of humpback whales, to establish hierarchies.

Many of the young of territorial fish, such as juvenile wrasse, surgeonfish, damselfish, butterflyfish and angelfish, use colour to reduce aggression. They adopt a different coloration from adults of the same species, in some cases so marked that the juveniles and adults were initially thought to belong to separate species. The very different hues stop the territorial adults viewing the juveniles as competitors, whether or not they are, and so they can live in relative harmony together, sharing the same patch of reef.

The communication by colour signals is probably even more subtle than this. As we observed on the Great Barrier Reef, many butterflyfish share territories in order to gain access to food and a ready partner. They typically move around in pairs, one following the other as they travel from coral to coral in search of food. Their narrow shape makes them difficult to see from behind. From the side they can be seen to have white, grey or yellow backgrounds, marked by lines and dots that make the fish less distinct the further away they are. In contrast to this camouflage, about 90 per cent of them have very conspicuous spots or patterns on the posterior part of their bodies, coloured yellow, red, orange or black. Some resemble eyes and may distract a predator away from the most vulnerable area, the head. The spot probably also acts as a moving signal to the following partner as the fish move over the reef. If the pair does happen to become separated, one will usually rise up in the water and tilt its body, allowing the light to catch its colours to maximum effect, thus attracting its partner's attention. The effectiveness of the signal between butterflyfish swimming along the reef is enhanced by the mark's position near the tail. As the leading fish moves its tail to and fro, the contrasting spots or patterns continually cross the line of vision of the following partner. The flashing or flicker effect produced might also confuse a predator approaching from behind.

Signalling may also be the function of the markings in groups of social fish. The stripes of sergeant majors probably help to synchronise swimming and feeding activities within the school. Like the territorial butterflyfish, over 90 per cent of schooling fish have a clear marking that moves as they swim and helps coordination within the group. In contrast, bottom-dwelling fish tend to have cryptic coloration, and the few which have conspicuous marks move them as little as possible.

The advantages of bright colours have to be balanced against the dangers of attracting predators and a compromise must be reached. The most common way of tempering overt colour signals is the gradation of dark backs to paler undersides,

The gloriously gilded juvenile reef triggerfish (*left*) bears little resemblance to the adult (*above*). They rejoice in the Hawaiian name of humuhumu-nukunuku-a-pua'a or 'the fish which carries a needle and has a snout and grunts like a pig'.

more commonly known as countershading. From below, the paler underside of the fish merges with the brightly lit surface and from above, the darker back is indistinct against the reef or the deep blue of open water. Many fish are countershaded to a greater or lesser degree, including the nocturnal squirrelfish. During the day this fish appears an even red colour, but at night the belly changes to a silvery-white. This is rarely seen by people, because when a torch is shone at squirrelfish their countershading disappears almost instantly. Countershading is very successful in reducing the risks of predation and it probably evolved in fish before any intricate patterns were superimposed.

Even the brilliantly coloured raccoon butterflyfish that we came across in Hawaii still retains its vital countershading. This fish's name comes from the black and white patterning of its head. The bright yellow of its underside darkens progressively up its flanks, and it sports a black spot just in front of the tail. The yellow fins, which make the body look larger than it actually is, are bordered by black. Its very attractive coloration becomes even more striking when one raccoon butterflyfish enters into a bout of aggression with another. By contracting and expanding the cells that house the pigments, both fish can become a much brighter yellow within seconds. The higher the intensity of aggression, the more dramatic the colour change and the greater the loss of countershading. The fish's behaviour changes too as they orientate themselves in parallel, with their heads at each other's tail. They circle in this position with fins erect, and lunge at and chase one another. During this clash, the important colour signals are given by the rear spot and the raised fins. The head to tail orientation means that each has an eye near the most conspicuously coloured part of its opponent. When they spread their fins, the dark lines bordering the dorsal, anal and tail fins join up to form a continuous black line. This both enlarges the outline of the fish and exaggerates by contrast the new brighter yellow hue. Furthermore, as the fish moves its tail in swimming, the line is repeatedly broken, producing the flicker or flashing effect.

The raccoon butterflyfish's strong visual signals are enhanced by countershading, for without its loss the colour change seen in these butterflyfish would be barely noticeable. As well as concealing the fish against predators, countershading also allows it to send signals which help to sort out social relationships, such as dominance hierarchies. Using their colours, fish can also defend their territories, thereby spacing themselves along a reef, maintain contact and synchronise behaviour within a group.

Fish communicate between as well as within species using colour. The best known example of such signalling is that of the cleaner fish. In the Indo-Pacific, cleaner wrasse typically have a black stripe running along their bodies which, towards the tail, broadens and is surrounded by a luminous blue. This, together with a characteristic way of swimming, attracts fish of all sizes which queue up to be cleaned. The same signals allow cleaner wrasse safe passage as they enter the mouths of giant groupers to remove food debris. In the Caribbean, a goby, not a member of the wrasse family, has adopted almost the same coloration of black stripe with blue border, and performs the same role. How the two species came to share the same colours is unclear. Presumably one established the signal and the other mimicked it, possibly through trial and error because cosmopolitan customers preferred cleaners with the characteristic contrasting stripe. Hawaiian cleaner wrasse perform the same tasks as those found elsewhere and are also of the same shape and bear a black stripe that widens near the tail. They too have bright edges to their tails, in this case pink.

If a signal confers an advantage, it will be copied and two species of blenny mimic cleaner fish. One has adopted the swimming technique of the wrasse, and both have developed the cleaner wrasse's shape and bright blue colour with a black horizontal line. So both appear to be soliciting customers for cleaning. These blennies are parasites, however, and instead of ridding their customers of unwanted scales or ectoparasites, they take chunks of flesh from the unsuspecting fish. The deceivers may in their turn be misled by deceptive coloration. These blennies prefer to attack the soft flesh of a fish's eye, but may be fooled into attacking the false eyespots borne by many fish, which are protected by tough scales.

Some fish use other ways of communicating besides visual signals, one of the more important of which is sound. Fish can hear as well as any other vertebrate within certain frequencies and use sound in a number of ways. Cod, sunfish, perch and many species of reef fish create sounds and communicate by them. One of the most obvious occasions when sound would prove useful is in courtship, and many male fish make noises to attract females. Freshwater male electric fish, for example, emit grunts, moans and growls that travel further in the water than their electric pulses and so are heard by more potential mates.

On the reef, many fish use sounds when spawning, and for defending their territories and their lives. Damselfish are among the more vocal, producing a range of sounds including chirps, grunts and pops. The various species of damselfish leave different intervals between the rapid pulses that make up the sounds and so each species makes a slightly different noise. Like the spotted dolphins of the Bahamas and the sperm whales of the Galápagos, damselfish have signature chirps by which each individual

Although brightly coloured the threadfin butterflyfish (*above*) and Tinker's butterflyfish (*below*) exhibit a degree of countershading whereby the upper body is shaded darker than the lower.

The milletseed butterflyfish (*above*) and the saddleback butterflyfish (*below*) produce a flicker-effect as they swim. Their tails beat across a contrasting colour which signals their whereabouts to a following partner.

can be recognised. Territorial damselfish use this chirp in defending their patch, for it is less effort to call a warning than to patrol the borders of the territory. While neighbouring damselfish of the same species will have familiar chirps, any intruder's chirp will be unfamiliar and the territory owner will respond aggressively.

Damselfish's signature chirps are also useful during courtship, for they enable a female to assess the size, and therefore the quality, of a male by the pitch of his call, the larger males producing deeper chirps. She can then both decide with whom she would like to spawn, and also determine the direction of the sound's origin up to a distance of 6–8 metres (20–26 feet) away. The chirping of a desirable male acts like a beacon, which the female will follow across the reef, passing over other, probably smaller, courting males on the way. By leaving her own area of reef and entering unfamiliar territory, the female is increasing her exposure to predation, but by heading straight for a chosen mate rather than wandering over the reef in search of one, she keeps danger to a minimum.

Triggerfish communicate by noise too, some producing sounds by grinding their front teeth together and others by using their modified pectoral fins. Each fin has a stout spine on its leading edge. The fish sweeps this back and forth over a soft membrane with very thin scales that lies just in front of an air bladder. Both pectoral fins move together to produce a drumming sound, typically heard as a series of volleys, which is surprisingly loud. Triggerfish drum when they get aggressive with one another, which is uncommon for they are usually widely spaced over the reef. When an encounter does occur, they quickly change colour to brighter hues, as the raccoon butterflyfish does. They also start producing volleys of drumming sounds, and these continue during the chase which often ensues. Triggerfish may use sound to communicate with predators as well as other triggerfish, because the noise they make is loud enough to be potentially startling. Being relatively slow swimmers, they need additional defences and so have tough bony plates for scales, and the trigger device by which they can lock themselves into crevices.

Another noisy marine creature is the pilot whale, which produces popping sounds and bird-like twitters amongst its echolocation clicks. Pilot whales, like killer whales, are large dolphins rather than true whales. The males reaching 6 metres (20 feet) or so in length and the females about 5 metres (16 feet). They are also called blackfish because of their almost total black colouring which is only interrupted by small areas of grey. By far their most distinctive feature is their very bulbous, round head which contains a waxy lump known as a melon. In older males the melon can become so large that it overhangs the whale's mouth.

Highly social animals, pilot whales live in groups of between ten and several hundred, often mixing with other species of dolphins, and use their acoustic abilities to maintain contact. But their loyalty and bonding to the group is sometimes their downfall. While many species of whale occasionally become stranded on beaches, the pilot whale is best known for doing so en masse. If one pilot whale swims ashore, all the others in the group will follow until they, too, are high and dry. They seem to survive overheating and sunstroke while the tide is out, but soon drown as the incoming water washes over their blow holes before they are able to shift themselves off the sand. The causes of such strandings are still unknown. It is thought that they may be due to parasite infestations of the ear, which decrease the whales' sense of balance and the effectiveness of their echolocation system. Or it may be that, being open water animals, they are confused by the echoes of their clicks returning from shallow bays. More recent research suggests that that may be disorientated by anomalies in the Earth's magnetic field which some whales are thought to use as a guide for navigation in certain places. If pilot whales use this field near unfamiliar coastlines, they may unwittingly follow a magnetic trail that leads them on to the shore.

Living in groups obviously also offers many advantages, including protection from predators. Pilot whales hunt in deep water for squid, their preferred prey. At other times they may be seen swimming in a very orderly fashion at a leisurely 7 km/h (4 mph), or resting at the surface. They bob at the surface as if very buoyant with their heads up or lie on their backs with their flippers held in the air. Secure in their groups, they may sleep and seem in no hurry to move off when disturbed. This relaxed attitude contrasts sharply with the wariness of some of the smaller inhabitants of the sea, which live under a more serious threat of predation.

Most reef fish actively try to avoid being eaten at all times. Many daytime fish have to feed throughout the sunlit hours and when they rest at night they shelter in a hole on the reef. Nocturnal fish tend to seek safety in a school, and it is common to see schooling squirrelfish and cardinalfish resting in caverns during the day. Activity on the reef appears to be greatest during the transition between day and night. Although at first sight the activity seems to be haphazard, careful observation reveals a well-defined sequence of events.

At the onset of dusk the smaller wrasse start to disappear and, about 15 minutes before sunset, the midwater plankton eaters, such as the sergeant major, drop down in the water. The smaller species are usually under cover well before sunset, while the larger species move progressively closer to the reef as the light dims. By this time

ABOVE: The clearly countershaded raccoon butterflyfish pales to reveal brighter yellows when in an aggressive encounter. BELOW: Hawaiian cleaner wrasse, with its notable pinkish tail stripes, attends to a tang.
RIGHT: The sociable and somewhat inquisitive pilot whale is easily distinguished by its bulbous head.

many species are migrating from one area of the reef to another, or from feeding grounds offshore on to the reef to sleep. Like commuters, they use the same paths each night, for by sticking to known routes in the company of so many other fish, the possibility of falling prey to a lurking predator is lessened. Aggression is frequent both within and between species, much of it relating to territorial disputes or social and feeding hierarchies. Surgeonfish, parrotfish and other species gather in mixed groups just above the reef, and mill around as the sun sets. Gradually, individuals leave the migrating schools and milling groups, and settle down on to the reef for the night.

About 10 to 15 minutes after sunset there is a sudden change and the fish disappear into the reef leaving the water apparently deserted. Looking closely at the reef, one can see pockets of activity as the butterflyfish and others jostle for prized sleeping sites, and the moorish idols swim close to the reef in small groups as they look for shelter. This period of calm is not quiet, for the noise on the reef increases as fish sort out their sleeping arrangements. As the daytime fish settle down, the nocturnal species begin to emerge from the caves and cracks now occupied by others. Cardinalfish come out first and mix with the remaining daytime fish close to the reef, and the early squirrelfish follow. Soon nocturnal fish emerge in great numbers and stream out on to the reef. Those squirrelfish that feed on off-shore plankton rise in the water column, gather into groups and migrate en masse to their feeding grounds.

Elsewhere in the world, this sequence of events is a response to the increased risk of predation at dusk. The lack of shallow-living groupers and snappers in Hawaii means that the threat is reduced there. Yet behaviour patterns to reduce the risk of predation, such as the smaller, more vulnerable fish seeking shelter first, still prevail. The responses are probably inherited from the original reef colonisers, and continue because they enhance the survival chances of those practising them.

Nocturnal fish migrating to their feeding areas suffer most as the last of the daylight silhouettes them for the few predators lurking below. Daytime fish also risk being taken if they are overly conspicuous. Most of them soften the contrasts they exhibit during the day, obliterating sharp lines, and mottling and blotching the clearer colours. The raccoon butterflyfish's yellow becomes a dullish brown, and the moorish idol's yellow and white flanks darken and a thin white bar develops within the black bar behind its eye.

Many daytime fish have established sleeping sites which they occupy night after night, while others have to acquire one nightly, often by fighting. The fish then need to ensure that they are well protected before they rest. As elsewhere, parrotfish in

Pyramid butterflyfish are brightly coloured by day (*above*), but assume darker shades for night-time protection (*below*).

Hawaii secrete a mucous cocoon and so does the Hawaiian cleaner wrasse, while most wrasse bury themselves in the sand. Butterflyfish may wedge themselves into rocks, but not as securely as the filefish. Relatives of the triggerfish, filefish have a similarly modified dorsal fin which they can use to lock themselves into a crevice. In addition, lowering a modified pelvic bone deepens the body to provide a second point of contact, and with their strong jaws and sharp chisel-like teeth they sometimes bite the rock, gaining a third anchor. Once in place, even a strong swell is unlikely to dislodge the sleeping filefish.

Pufferfish are better protected from predators. As well as their famous ability to swell up when attacked, pufferfish contain the poison tetraodontoxin in their skin and flesh. They are considered a delicacy by many people but extremely careful preparation of the fish is required to prevent the poison contaminating the food. Their toxicity seems to vary with area and species, and while in Japan a number of people die each year from eating pufferfish, few deaths have been reported in Hawaii. The sharpnose pufferfish, or tobies, have scales like velcro, giving them a certain purchase on the rock, and they secrete a glue that attaches them to the reef. Firmly stuck and poisonous, they can rest secure at night.

Plankton rise from the reef at night and are attracted in their millions to light, whether from the torches of divers or from buildings close to the shore. On the Kona coast, on the west side of the Big Island, the lights of a hotel attract not only plankton but also manta rays which come to feast on them. Mantas, or devil fish, are benign rays which feed on minute fish and plankton in surface waters. They cruise through the ocean with their gaping mouths wide open and filter out the food. Mantas can grow to immense proportions, weiging up to 1400 kilograms (3100 pounds) and having a 'wing' span of about 7 metres (23 feet). They swim by beating their huge 'wings' slowly through the water, rather like a large bird of prey in flight. They usually inhabit the open ocean and are only occasionally encountered by divers when they come inshore in search of swarming plankton.

The bizarre juxtaposition of such a creature and a hotel complex in Hawaii is just one of the signs that there, as elsewhere, humans are increasingly encroaching on an otherwise pristine wilderness. When the first Polynesians ventured forth from the Marquesas Islands over 1500 years ago and discovered Hawaii, they found untouched forests covering the landscape. The human colonists began to replace the indigenous trees with coconuts and sugar cane, for few of the plants there bore food for them. They also brought pigs and fowl with them, and began to fish the sea.

This relative harmony was interrupted when Captain James Cook arrived at the islands in 1778. He came at a time when the islanders were celebrating the harvest and, greeting him as a reincarnation of the god of harvest, Lono, they showed him exceptional hospitality. But when he returned to the islands a year later to make good some storm damage, a dispute broke out over the theft of a cutter and tempers flared. Cook was stabbed in the resulting melee on the shores of Kealakekua Bay on Big Island, whilst trying to stop his men from firing at the islanders. His legacy remains, however, for with him he brought goats and disease-carrying sailors, both of which have had an impact.

Syphilis spread fast among the Hawaiians, and subsequent colonists brought epidemics of smallpox, measles and influenza. The combined effects of these were to reduce the human population from 300 000 to only 50 000 within a century. The hardy goats were ruinous as they wandered over the islands in their thousands, browsing on trees and grazing grass down to the roots. More recent introductions, such as cardinal birds, sparrows, egrets, cattle and prickly pears, have also wreaked havoc among the vulnerable endemic animals and plants. Even today, about 30 new species of insect are brought in unwittingly each year with the flood of tourists that visit the islands.

Many of the tourists are divers, for the water enthusiasts, once restricted to the tiled hotel swimming pool, are now encouraged to explore the ocean. Numbers of sport fishermen, snorkellers, divers and whale-watchers are booming, and they bring in over US $280 million to Hawaii annually. Diving in Hawaii is an established part of the tourist industry and gives great pleasure to many, but its effects on the more popular reefs are numerous. Carelessly thrown anchors break coral that has taken many years to grow and kicked flippers can cause extensive damage. Corals and sponges are trampled on, and shells are collected, to be replaced by cups, cans, plastic bags, glass and bottles left scattered over the sea floor. The development that comes with increasing indigenous populations and tourism adds siltation, sewage, industrial waste and agricultural run-off to the inevitable litter.

Even in established marine parks, where spearfishing and coral collection is prohibited, the reef is often sacrificed in the interest of attracting the attention of 'naturalists'. One such park is Molokini Crater, a semi-submerged crater off the west coast of Maui. It is said that a ring of suntan oil marks the crater's jagged rim. In peak season, 35 or so boats spill 1000 divers and snorkellers daily into the protected

OVERLEAF: Huge but harmless, manta rays feed only on plankton. Water is channelled through their cavernous mouths and the tiny organisms sieved out.

waters, making them as crowded with people as with fish. Diving time is limited in the crater because as the day proceeds the winds increase, and the water becomes too rough for the boats. In the short time available to them, though, people have a great impact. We went there to see the spectacle, and were amazed by the number of fish that swarmed around us. They have been fed by so many people for so long that they are on their way to becoming a nuisance in their quest for free food. Lemon or milletseed butterflyfish teemed in their hundreds, obliterating the other divers around us and the snorkellers above. But we had no food for them and gradually they dispersed to more lucrative areas. Moray eels were being fed by nervous divers not used to proximity with such creatures and worried by the stories of people being bitten. Quieter spots can be found around the crater, and from the comparatively untouched outer rim we caught a glimpse of a hammerhead shark, and a green sea turtle flapped its ungainly way past us.

Robert Runcie, when Archbishop of Canterbury, said that tourism shows a 'wholesale disregard for indigenous lifestyles'. Although referring to indigenous people, this comment describes equally the effect of tourism on fish and other marine creatures. For example, in their desire to see marine animals close up, divers will feed them anything that comes to hand. At one time, divers would cut up sea urchins to watch the feeding frenzy that ensued. This practice largely stopped when people realised the important role sea urchins play in keeping the algal growth down and thereby allowing corals to grow. Now processed cheese, bread and unwanted hot dogs are just a few of the delicacies offered to opportunistic fish. Junk food is particularly bad for fish because it contains saturated animal fats that, at the temperature of seawater, will solidify and clog up inside them. Marine creatures contain unsaturated liquid fats that are not affected by the cold in the same way. Specially developed fish food sticks are now being manufactured, although some still contain animal fats. Another problem is the litter that accompanies most fish feeding dives. Inevitably the bait is carried down in a bag of some sort and, with such eager and impatient fish around, the bag is often forgotten by the diver and eaten along with the bait.

Human actions also rebound on people in many ways, the most obvious being the aggressiveness of fish wanting to be fed. Sergeant majors may nip an ear lobe in their impetuous greed and, more seriously, the barracudas and virtually blind moray eels may accidentally take an extended finger instead of the proffered titbit, while sharks have bitten many a diver. One diver was even killed by a grouper at Cod Hole on the Great Barrier Reef when the huge fish swam at him and knocked him unconscious, causing him to drown.

On the positive side, such close encounters often dispel prejudices against sharks, barracudas and morays. Also, as land-based consumers, we tend to be unaware of the silent plight of the reefs. Seeing marine creatures and touching them often heightens people's awareness of the needs of such animals, and increases overall concern about the underwater environment. The damage could be lessened in the future by stricter control of entry to the reef. Isolating the impact of tourism to a few selected areas would allow people to appreciate the beauty of the reefs while leaving the greater whole relatively unharmed.

One way of seeing the reef without creating much disturbance is by submarine. The submarine pilots make sure their vessel never touches or damages the reef, and there are no flippers to kick the corals. Hawaii offers excursions in submarines that take 46 passengers down on to the natural reef and, more recently, on to a sunken ship. There are also plans to sink an aeroplane and a truly artificial reef made of concrete and fibre glass. Marine life quickly colonises and takes refuge in such structures. Artificial reefs in unprotected areas can do more harm than good for they attract fish that would otherwise remain dispersed, and this greater concentration makes them more vulnerable to fishermen. The wreck has been placed in an area that has been heavily overfished, and it is hoped that the abundance of reef animals will increase around the carefully chosen site. If the site is protected, the fish populations will increase on the artificial reef and will, in time, spread out over previously inhabited areas and further enrich the sea.

Without scuba gear, and with no risk of encountering unrecognised dangerous animals or experiencing decompression sickness, enthusiasts can enjoy the reef as it is at 50 metres (160 feet) depth through portholes that line the sides of the submarine. The vessel also makes night dives, floodlighting the realm of the invertebrates. In just one of the submarines working off the Hawaiian islands, over 300 people a day venture into the sea and the submarine is out seven days a week. Those unfamiliar with the inhabitants of a reef are told about reef ecology and so these trips help to increase knowledge and understanding of the reef as much as, if not more than, any amount of sport diving.

The submarine industry is booming, and a predicted 60 submarines for tourists will be in operation around the world in the next few years. Scientists also use them because, although expensive, submarines provide a much less traumatic way of assessing fish stocks than trawling. Such assessments are becoming more necessary as our fishing techniques increase in efficiency and our over-exploitation of the ocean continues. One development which may help to reduce our depredations is aquaculture.

LEFT: Molokini Crater, a lifesized aquarium for aquatic tourists. RIGHT: I was welcomed into Molokini's waters by expectant butterflyfish; they have been conditioned by over-generous divers.

Integrated freshwater and seawater fish ponds have probably been in use in Hawaii for over 1500 years. Today, the freshwater farming includes prawns living in flooded lava pools, and carp and mullet ponds, the waste water from which is used to irrigate papaya, banana and avocado crops. Seawater farming has become a well-integrated system. From 600 metres (2000 feet) down off the Kona coast, polythene pipes bring 75 000 litres (16 500 gallons) per minute of cold oceanic water up to the surface and on to land at Keahole Point, where some of it flows into ponds. The advantages of this deep water are many. It contains little or no sediment and bacteria, and no phytoplankton as they cannot live at such lightless depths. So there are no unwanted plankton blooms and diseases to threaten the growth of sensitive creatures in the ponds. The cold water, at a temperature of 6°C (43°F), can easily be warmed to the precise optimum temperature by exposure to the surrounding air, which is usually at a temperature of around 22°C (72°F). So any plant or animal that requires a water temperature of between, say, 10 and 22°C (50 and 72°F) can be accommodated. The water is also rich in nutrients, providing the essential ingredients for plants to photosynthesise. Warm surface water is also piped in for use in the system.

With nutrients and sunshine to keep it going, kelp grows exceptionally well in the ponds at Keahole Point. The oxygen it produces during the day through photosynthesis aerates the water to the benefit of salmon living alongside the kelp. The waste from the salmon, in turn, acts as a fertiliser for both the kelp and the planktonic creatures that begin to grow in the water. Oysters are also cultured in ponds, and these keep the water clean by filter-feeding the clouding plankton. Any phytoplankton brought in with the warm surface water and not eaten by the oysters are taken by abalone larvae. The adult abalone that develop have less shell and more meat than in the wild and are fed kelp. So, too, are the sea urchins which are grown for their roe, exported primarily to Japan. All these animals are harvested periodically as they reach marketable size, and it is expected that, in time, 1–1.5 million salmon and 0.5–1 million abalone and sea urchins will be sold each year.

The threatened giant clam we saw in Australia is now being farmed in Hawaii. Since the algae living within it need only nutrient-rich water and sunlight, the clam grows well in the warm surface water piped in from the sea. There is also a plan to produce 500 000 lobsters a year, all year round. Maine lobsters, hitherto a seasonal treat, are hatched and grown in an exact mix of cold and warm water. While they take seven years to reach a weight of 2 kilograms (4.4 pounds) in the sea, they take a mere two years to do so in this refined environment.

Seaweeds flourish too and are marketed as sea vegetables. Nori, a seaweed used to wrap sushi, is a particular favourite in Japan and increasingly popular in Hawaii. After some experimentation, it was found, predictably, that the conditions in which nori grows best are the same as those found in its natural home in Japan. Both nori and ogo, a Hawaiian seaweed, grow so rapidly they have to be harvested every week.

Also cultured are microscopic algae that grow so fast they have to be stirred constantly by paddles to keep an even rate of photosynthesis within the crop. One called spirulina is harvested twice a week and sold as a health food product in Europe, America and Japan. Another produces beta carotene, also found in far smaller concentrations in carrots. This chemical is highly sought after for it is a source of vitamin A and is believed to help arrest certain types of cancer.

The cold water is put to diverse uses other than aquaculture. It services the air-conditioning of the buildings surrounding the marine farms. It also plays a part in an ingenious agricultural system. Cold water pipes running both underground and just above the ground allow the culturing of temperate plants, such as strawberries, lettuces and asparagus. The plants fare much better with their roots cooled by the underwater pipes, the strawberries for example having a sugar content five times as high as they would with their roots at ambient temperatures. The cold of the pipes above ground causes water to condense on them which drips on to the growing plants, watering them.

Most extraordinary of all is that these interdependent aquaculture, air-conditioning and agricultural systems are by-products of one of the major uses of the water – electricity generation through a technique known as OTEC (Ocean Thermal Energy Conversion). This uses the difference in temperature between the sun-warmed surface waters and the cold inflow to generate power. OTEC could be of great interest in our energy hungry world because we are using up the fossil fuels, such as coal and oil, which currently produce most of our electrical energy.

Similarly aquaculture has enormous potential in our increasingly populated world. Aquaculture now accounts for 10 per cent of our harvest of marine organisms worldwide, and by the year 2000 it is expected to be providing between five and ten times the present amount. If people elsewhere in the world can be persuaded to eat marine foods other than fish, as they do in Japan, the pressures on the oceans will greatly decrease. The marriage of energy production and aquaculture at Keahole

OVERLEAF, LEFT: Spinner dolphins, sleek and elegant, cannot resist playing in the bow waves of boats.
RIGHT: Leaping spinner dolphin, at one with the ocean.

Point is particularly exciting, for it suggests that, with careful management, the oceans could fulfil more of our food and energy needs. It also shows that we might be able to exploit ocean resources effectively without wholesale destruction, leaving much of the ocean for its inhabitants and ourselves to enjoy.

We were reminded of the importance of this when, standing by the OTEC plant at Keahole Point, we looked out to sea and saw spinner dolphins leaping. These social animals often gather with other species of dolphins and whales in schools of thousands. Their name comes from their habit of leaping high into the air and spinning around and around. These exuberant antics do not seem to be performed to remove parasites or escape predators as the dolphins will leap and spin under any conditions. One dolphin twisting and spinning sets the others off. We could only surmise that they are expressing a pure *joie de vivre*.

INDEX